The Spell
on the Stones

Westminster Press Books by
ELIZABETH P. FLEMING

Gift from the Mikado
Redcloud & Co.
The Spell on the Stones

The Spell
on the Stones

By

ELIZABETH P. FLEMING

Illustrated by
GEORGEANN HELMS

THE WESTMINSTER PRESS
PHILADELPHIA

LIBRARY OF CONGRESS CATALOG CARD NO. 61–7704

PRINTED IN THE UNITED STATES OF AMERICA

To
JOHN

1

DAVID TRENT SAT BESIDE MISS MOONEY IN THE AIR terminal at New York International Airport waiting for the bus that would take them to their flight gate. Crowds were passing to and fro, porters laden with bags led passengers to the different airline offices, loud-speakers blared. Even though David hadn't wanted to take this trip, he had to admit the terminal was an exciting place.

" Who wants to go to Ireland? " he had demanded when his mother had first spoken of it. " All the fellows are going to Scout camp. I'd be the only one not there."

" Och," said his mother. Usually she talked the same as anyone else does, only maybe more prettily, but whenever she was really in earnest, her speech lapsed into a soft brogue. "It's not every boy of eleven who has the chance to fly to Ireland to spend the summer on his grandmother's farm. Someday you'll be thinking you were the lucky one to go at all."

David shook his head, and his mother didn't say any more just then. But that wasn't the end of it. Every time a letter came from Ireland she brought up the subject again. It was all because Aunt Annie, his

7

mother's sister, had made up her mind to go to Alaska and marry James Mackie, who was homesteading there. Her mother, who was Grandmother Hazlett, was dead set against it. It wasn't that she had anything against James Mackie — the Mackies and the Hazletts had been friends for years — but Alaska was too far away and too cold altogether. Didn't the Americans call it an icebox when they bought it? " Alaska, indeed! " said Grandmother Hazlett. But Annie had made up her mind, and nothing could stop her. It had come to the point that the two of them were scarcely speaking. Angry letters came to America. Grandmother said that Annie was a selfish, foolish girl who didn't know her own mind, and Annie said it was her mother who was the selfish one. She wasn't going to ruin her entire life for anyone.

" The pity of it is I can see both sides," sighed David's mother.

" Your mother has never forgiven me for carrying you off to America," said her husband. " She doesn't want another daughter to desert her."

" That's what makes it hard," Mrs. Trent agreed. " I'm so far away. She's never even seen her only grandson." David's mother looked proudly at him.

Of course, David knew all about how his dad had met his mother when he had been in Ireland on business. They had fallen in love and married, and Grandmother Hazlett hadn't liked it a bit, though she and Dad were good friends now.

" If it weren't such a long way, we'd send David to visit her," said his mother. " It would be a comfort to her. Why not? " she asked suddenly. " He could fly.

8

It's nothing to fly these days. How would you like to fly to Ireland, Davy, darling? "

" Who? Me? " asked David in alarm.

" Yes, you," said his mother.

" For Pete's sake," David burst out. " I don't have to go clear to Ireland just so someone can get married, do I? People get married all the time."

His mother only smiled at him, and his father didn't say anything. David hoped they might forget all about it. But after that, his mother kept talking about Ireland and things that had happened when she had lived there as a girl.

" My fuchsias aren't doing very well," she would say, looking at some ragged plants in the window. " At Grandmother Hazlett's there's a fuchsia hedge covered with red and purple flowers. The beauty of it would go to your heart." Or his mother would talk about the kitchen in the Hazlett farmhouse. " The big fireplace takes up almost the whole side of the room, and the turf fire burns there day in and day out. Oh, the good smell of burning turf! Over the fireplace hang two old guns, and under them is the stone ax your grandfather found in the bog."

" In the bog? " asked David, interested in spite of himself. " That's a silly place to find anything."

" It's a splendid place," said his mother. " It's full of all kinds of things — old leather clothes and wooden bowls preserved for hundreds of years. But the ax is a real relic. It's older than history, they say. Years and years before Ireland even had a name some early man lost his ax in the bog, and there it lay until one day your grandfather found it. You'll see it when you go."

9

"Oh, Mom," said David, " you like that ax more than I do. You go to Ireland instead of me."

"And leave your father!" she cried. "I couldn't do it. But you can go. Your grandmother needs to see her only grandson."

David groaned. But what could he say when his mother had made up her mind? It looked pretty hopeless. His mother was talking again.

"Those long-ago people set up great stone monuments too. There's one at old John Steenson's place — three stones side by side, and another laid across the top. No one knows what the monuments are for or how the stones were ever hoisted into place. The children used to say that the stones were men who had been bewitched, and that when the moon was right, they danced together."

"Now you're kidding," David said.

"I never saw them dance," said his mother, smiling.

"And there's a big mound in the middle of John Steenson's field, built by the same people," she went on. "They say there's a crock of gold buried in it."

"Why don't they dig there and find the gold?" asked David.

"The story is that there's a spell on it," said his mother.

"A spell? That's silly," said David. "I'd like to dig there. We could use a pot of gold." His eyes were sparkling at the thought.

"It's only a story," said his mother. "There are plenty of stories in Ireland."

Then the day came when Mrs. Trent announced that Miss Mooney, the school nurse, who came from

County Wicklow, was flying home to Ireland for the summer. " She says she'll be glad to look after David, and his Uncle Robert can meet him at Shannon," said Mrs. Trent.

It was decided just like that. David didn't have a word to say about it, that is, a word that did any good. He said plenty, but his mother didn't seem to hear him. When it was time for him to go, though, she looked sober. " It's only for the summer," said Mr. Trent to comfort her, but he looked sober too.

" Good-by, Davy, darling," said his mother in a smothered voice. They were still waving when the train pulled out of the station. Just to think about it made a lump come up in David's throat.

So here he was sitting with Miss Mooney in the air terminal. They had been here a long time because Miss Mooney had been afraid of being late. David had made the rounds of the overseas airlines and had looked at the books in the bookshop, but they were mostly in foreign languages, and there wasn't a single comic book there.

" I can't make out a word they're saying over the loud-speakers," said Miss Mooney.

David listened. " Shannon — Ahm-ster-dahm."

He sat up. " That's ours," he said.

" Platform eleven, please," the voice went on.

Miss Mooney was in a great flurry. It was David who led the way to the gate where a bus waited.

" Be careful now," said Miss Mooney to the bus driver.

" Lady," he said, " I've been driving this bus for six years and never had an accident yet."

11

They were on their way past blocks of great apartment buildings, set close together. Where do the kids play? David wondered. The bus came to open fields, and hangars, and planes taking off and landing. The loud-speakers were blaring again when they got off the bus. " Shannon, Ahm-ster-dahm — Gate 2, please."

Miss Mooney caught David's hand and started off at a jog trot. Holding tight together, they hurried through the gate, down a long corridor, around a corner and down a ramp, until they came to a man who examined their tickets and waved them through another gate. There was the plane, with a pretty girl waiting at the steps to welcome them. Miss Mooney sank into a seat. " We made it! " she panted.

David looked around. A lighted sign read: " Fasten your seat belts. No smoking, please." The engines exploded into sound, and the plane began to move. It taxied across the field, gaining speed. Then with a roar it rose into the air. Presently, the captain's voice announced, " Below you is the Statue of Liberty."

" That little thing! " cried David.

"It seems little because we're up so high," said Miss Mooney, who had recovered her breath and was looking down over his shoulder. " It's a grand sight as you're coming in on a ship. I'll never forget it."

After a while dinner was served on trays on which all the dishes were set in slots to prevent their sliding about. Later the lights were dimmed, and the hostess showed David how to let down his seat so he was almost lying down. It seemed he had scarcely closed his eyes when Miss Mooney was shaking him.

" Wake up! " she said. " We're almost there."

Through the window he could see a checkerboard of green, green fields. " The Emerald Isle," said Miss Mooney.

His Uncle Robert, who was no older than the counselors at camp, was waiting for him. " Call me Robert," he said and gave David a friendly clap on the back. They all went together to collect their bags and then Miss Mooney said good-by.

David never remembered much about the ride to his grandmother's. He dozed uncomfortably most of the way on the train, and Robert didn't try to make him talk. But there was a great welcome at the end of the journey. His grandmother, Aunt Annie, Mary McInnelly, who was the housemaid, and Ownie Kern, the hired boy, were all waiting for him. Tired as he was, he could still see that Annie was young and very pretty. Grandmother Hazlett was straight and spare, with white hair done in a bun on the back of her head, but her eyes were bright blue like his mother's.

" Welcome to Slieverow House, lad dear," she said and gave him a welcoming kiss.

The table was set in the kitchen before the great fireplace, and they all sat down to tea but he was too sleepy to eat. His head kept nodding, then he would sit up with a jerk, only to nod again.

" He's fair perished for sleep," said Mary McInnelly.

"You can go to bed right now if you like," said Annie. " You are to have the settle bed in the kitchen, and here is your dressing room." She opened a door beside the fireplace to show a tiny room with a dresser and a washbowl and pitcher. There was a row of pegs on the wall above. " For your clothes," she told him.

13

He got into his pajamas and fell into the lovely softness of his bed. Once he roused to hear voices. " Going to Alaska by yourself like any servingmaid," said his grandmother. " James Mackie should think shame to himself to do no better for his bride."

" But the expense of it," said Annie. " It would cost enough to buy all our furniture if James came after me."

" He'd come after you if he was worthy of a Hazlett," said her mother, " and that's my last word on it."

" I hope it is," flared Annie and began to cry.

" Hark, you'll wake the child," said her mother.

They went away then and David, too tired to think, fell asleep once more.

14

2

IT WAS BROAD DAYLIGHT WHEN DAVID WOKE TO A pleasant smell of burning in the air. Peat, he thought, sniffing. Mary McInnelly was raking the turf in the fireplace into a glowing heap. Then she hung the kettle over it. There was a cookstove in the room, but David was to find that Mary liked the big fireplace best. He lay looking around him. There were the two old guns over the fireplace, just as his mother had said, and that queer thing hanging beneath must be the ax that was found in the bog. The outside door was cut into two parts, and the upper half was open. Through it he could see the fuchsia hedge covered with blossoms. He wished his mother were here to see it.

Robert came down the stairs and went out through the half door. Then David heard his grandmother's step on the stair, and he slid out of bed. The dressing room was dark, and he left the door open a crack while he got into his clothes. He washed in the washbowl and, shivering a little, pulled his sweater over his head.

The family were at breakfast when he came out. His grandmother gave him a good-morning kiss, and Mary McInnelly ran to get his porridge.

15

"It's cold today," he said.

"Cold?" asked his grandmother in surprise.

"Not a bit of it," said Robert. Ownie Kern shook his head.

"I'm fair perished with the heat, myself," said Mary McInnelly. Her cheeks were as red as apples. She looked as though she could never be cold.

"I'm afraid your blood is too thin," said his grandmother. "Lad dear, you're as pale as buttermilk."

David flushed. He didn't like such talk, but Annie came into the room just then, so no more was said. This morning she was prettier than ever in a trim tweed suit, but her eyes looked as though she had been crying.

"All dressed up," said her brother.

"I've decided to go to Armagh to visit Sheila Steele," said Annie, not looking at her mother.

"And when did you make up your mind to this?" asked Mrs. Hazlett.

"Last night," said Annie shortly.

David remembered then the talk he had overheard. Annie and her mother were angry with each other all right. He didn't dare look up, but he seemed to feel angry thoughts whirling about. No one said anything for a minute, then Robert turned to David.

"Do you see the old ax over the fireplace?" he asked.

David nodded. "My mother told me about it," he said. "Grandfather found it in the bog, didn't he?"

"He did," said Robert, "and a fine relic it is, fit to be in a museum, they say. Some man lost it in the bog thousands of years ago, and there it lay until your grandfather found it when he was cutting turf."

16

" May I please go and look at it? " David asked his grandmother.

" Of course you may," she told him.

He went over to the fireplace to stare at the queer-looking thing hanging there. It was a smooth, polished piece of stone thrust through a blackened branch that made a sort of handle. It didn't look like any ax David had ever seen. Everyone seemed to be very proud of it. He hardly knew what to say, but Annie saved him.

"Colonel McClintock of Bride's Hill would give anything for that ax," she said.

Two red spots came out on Mrs. Hazlett's face. " He can never have it," she said. " That ax is to hang over the hearth as long as there's a Hazlett living at Slieve-row House."

When Mary McInnelly and Ownie Kern had left the table, Mrs. Hazlett turned to Annie. " How long do you intend to stay at Armagh? " she asked.

" I'll let you know," said Annie. " Robert, will you drive me to the station? My bag is packed. I'll be ready in ten minutes."

Robert looked unhappy. " Well now, Annie," he began, " do you think — "

" I don't think. I know," said Annie and left the room.

" Get the car," said Mrs. Hazlett. " The lad can go with you. Would you like to go for a ride, David? "

" Yes," said David, glad to get away from the unpleasantness.

When Annie came down with her suitcase, she gave her mother a kiss on the cheek. "I'll write," she said and went out to the car. It was a little one, but all three of them fitted into the front seat. Mrs. Hazlett stood at the half door, a lonely figure.

" It's too bad," said Robert.

" It is," said Annie, " but all we're doing is snapping at each other. It's best to get away for a while. Only, I hate to leave David just as he gets here." She smiled at him.

" You won't stay long? " asked Robert.

" I won't," she promised.

" I guess it's cold in Alaska," David ventured after a while. " It's colder there than it is here even."

" It's not cold here," laughed Annie. " Summers in Alaska are fine," she went on. " The days are so long that there's plenty of time for things to grow even if the season is short. James writes he's going to have a fine potato crop."

" Potatoes grow all right here," said Robert.

Annie flared up at that. " Are you against me too? " she cried.

" No, no, but it's hard on Mother — "

" I know," said Annie and wiped her eyes, " but I can't have her always talking against James."

When the train had gone with Annie aboard, Robert said they would do some shopping. The people in the store crowded around them. " So this is Mary Hazlett's lad," they said. " And hasn't he the Hazlett look about him with the blue eyes of him, and all! And how is your mother? I mind she was a dear, wee lass, always with a smile for everyone."

On the way home they saw two horsemen riding across an open field. They waved, then sailed gracefully over a hedge, and disappeared from sight. " That's

Colonel McClintock and his daughter, Lynn," said Robert. "You'll be seeing more of them. Lynn is a great little horsewoman. She'll be riding in the point-to-point one day."

"What's that?" asked David.

"It's the great spring race," Robert told him. "It comes in March. It's a pity you won't be here to see it."

"I don't know anything about riding," said David. "Are there any boys around here?"

"Aye, there's Denny Foley. He'll be coming over to see you. You'll find plenty to do here, never fear."

But when they reached home and Robert hurried off to the fields, David wondered what he was going to do with himself. He walked slowly toward the house, feeling strange and lonely.

"Oh, there you are," said his grandmother. "Mary McInnelly is going to take lunch to the men in the fields at noon, and I thought you could both eat with them." David's face brightened. The thought of a picnic made him feel better. "Look about the place a bit while you're waiting for Mary," his grandmother finished.

David went to the barn first, which Robert called the byre. There were stalls for the animals but they were empty now. The horses were in the hayfield, and the cows and the donkey were out at pasture. In the middle of the yard was a pump with the head of a lion. When David moved the pump handle, water poured out of the lion's mouth. The fuchsia hedge ran the length of the yard. Behind it was a flat stone, and David sat there to wait for Mary McInnelly. She came at last with the lunch in a wicker basket.

19

" You can give me a hand with the creel, Davy, lad," she said. So carrying the basket between them, they started off for the field.

Mary was happy to be going on a picnic and laughed and joked all the way to the hayfield. Neat haystacks stood in rows down the field, and just as David and Mary came into sight, Robert took a running jump straight up the side of a stack to stand upright on the top. When he saw David he flapped his arms. " Cock-a-doodle-do," he crowed.

David burst out laughing. " Can I come up there too? " he cried.

" And why not? " said Robert. Leaning over, he gripped David by the hand and hauled him to the top of the stack.

Mary McInnelly set down the creel and picked up a pitchfork, and she and Ownie Kern began pitching hay to Robert who spread it by hand over the top of the stack — David helping as best he could. When the hay was stacked, Robert leaped lightly to the ground, and David slid down bringing some of the hay along with him. " I'm sorry," he apologized, but Robert only smiled. " Think nothing of it," he said.

They ate their lunch in the shade of the blackthorn hedge. There were rolls of soda bread — " farls," Robert called them — and black currant jam and fresh buttermilk and strong black tea. David had never tasted such strong tea before and couldn't help making a face at the bitter taste.

" If it's too strong," said Mary McInnelly, " take more sugar in it."

" Tea is good for you," said Ownie Kern. " It'll

brush the cobwebs out of your head." They called Ownie the hired boy, but he was really a grown man, much older than Robert. Robert and he did all the farm work, but it was really Grandmother Hazlett who gave the orders. Everyone did exactly as she said.

"It's nice out here," said David, looking happily about. The sun had grown warm. He took off his sweater and laid it on the grass beside him.

"You like eating outdoors?" asked Robert.

David nodded. "We eat out a lot at home," he said. "We have an outdoor grill in the back yard, and Dad cooks on it. Mom says he can broil a steak better than she can. I can cook too. Hot dogs," he finished proudly.

Mary gave a squeal. "Do they eat dogs in America?" she cried.

David laughed. "Not real dogs. Wieners," he explained. "We have a dog too. When Dad broils a steak, Crackers just sits there and wags his tail and waits for snacks. He has very good manners and he's smart too. He knows every word that's said to him."

"Aye, a dog is a very intelligent beast," said Ownie.

Mary sighed. "Miss Annie must be well on the way to Armagh," she said. "Dear help her. The course of true love never did run smooth."

" 'Tis a rocky road to Alaska," said Ownie.

"I'd take it any time for my true love," said Mary.

"Would you now?" said Ownie. "Not I. I'd as lief lay me down at the Dark Angle as go off to that perishing place."

"What's the Dark Angle?" asked David.

"Many's the strange goings on there," said Ownie.

"What kind of goings on?" David persisted.

21

Ownie looked over his shoulder and lowered his voice. " They do say that at the dark of the moon the Little People meet there."

David looked from one face to the other. Ownie was serious, and Mary's face was solemn. Robert got to his feet.

" Don't be giving the lad such tales," he said, " besides, it's high time we got back to our work."

Mary McInnelly reluctantly packed the remains of the lunch, and she and David started for home while the men went back to the haymaking.

" Mary," said David as they walked along, " who are the Little People? "

" Och," said Mary, " and how can I tell? The Little People are here and they're there. Sometimes they're good, and sometimes they're terrible bad. It's best to have nothing to do with them. But sometimes you can't help yourself at all."

" You're making up stories," said David.

" I am not," said Mary McInnelly. " Sure I wouldn't lie to you. But mind now, lad, don't be speaking to your grandmother of it. She doesn't hold with the Little People at all."

3

DAVID SAT ON THE STONE BESIDE THE FUCHSIA HEDGE
wondering what to do with himself. He felt a little for-
lorn. Everyone was busy, with no time for him. He
tried to think what might be happening at home. Six
hours' difference in time made it hard to figure out.
Probably most of the kids were just having breakfast.
Then maybe they'd go to the swimming pool or have
a game of catch. They wouldn't be going to camp until
next week. If it was hot, his mother would make lem-
onade. He felt very far away from them all.

A boy was coming down the road, a boy with a good-
natured, freckled face and a mop of untidy red hair.
" Hi," said David.

The boy stopped and grinned at him. He wasn't
much older than David. " Hello," he said, " and how
was America when you were leaving it? "

" How did you know I came from America? " asked
David.

" Sure everyone knows that," said the boy, " but I
could tell it anyway by the cut of your boots."

David looked down at his sneakers and then at the
boy's stout boots, and they both began to laugh.

23

"My name's Denny Foley," said the boy.

"And mine's David Trent. My uncle told me about you. Are there any more kids around here?"

"Well, now, there's Lynn McClintock over at Bride's Hill," said Denny.

"She's a girl," said David.

"She can do anything a boy can," said Denny, "and she's a grand horsewoman."

"That wouldn't do me any good," grumbled David. "I don't know anything about horses."

"You always ride in motor cars in America," said Denny. "You never walk at all."

"Who told you that?" asked David. "Of course we walk. I can walk as far as you can."

"Come on, then," said Denny. "I'm just on my way to visit Old McManus. It's no more than a mile."

"I'll have to tell my grandmother first," said David. But when they went to the house there was no one about. Mary McInnelly was off somewhere, and David remembered that his grandmother always took a nap in the afternoon. He found a piece of paper and wrote a note as he did at home when his mother was out. "Gone with Denny Foley," he wrote. "Love, David."

It was the longest mile David had ever walked. They went on and on up hill and down dale. "Do you call this only a mile?" he asked at last.

"An Irish mile," said Denny.

"I don't think my grandmother will like it if I'm late for supper — tea, I guess you call it here," said David.

Denny gave an impatient hitch to his trousers. The Foleys never worried about being late for tea. "I'll get you back in time for your tea," he promised. "Here

24

we are. Old McManus lives down this lane." He plunged off the road into what looked to David like a tangle of weeds and brambles.

"Are you sure this is a lane?" asked David, looking ahead into a gloomy thicket where the overhanging branches seemed to shut out the sunlight. "I don't think you've got the right place."

"I have," said Denny crossly. "Come on, now," and he gave a jerk to his head.

Denny went ahead, but they made slow progress. It had been a long time since anyone had gone that way. They tripped over vines and fallen branches, and nettles stung their hands and faces. "I don't believe you know where you're going," said David.

"I do," said Denny. But he didn't sound happy.

A hare darted across the path in front of them and turned to stare in a knowing way. A rustle sounded in the bushes. Denny stopped in his tracks. "They do say that the Little People use this path," he said.

David was close behind. He had to stop too. "Little People?" he said. "You mean fairies? You don't believe in them, do you?"

"Hold your whist," said Denny sharply, looking around as though afraid there might be listeners.

"My grandmother doesn't believe in them —" David began.

"Och, your grandmother," said Denny. "Your grandmother doesn't know everything that goes on in Ireland."

Soon they came out into a clearing where a tiny thatched cottage stood in the middle of a garden. There were sweet William, and bachelor's-button, and pink and scarlet poppies, and beside the door, a green bush.

"That's a leek bush," said Denny. "It keeps the house from burning down." He was himself again. "Hello, the house!" he shouted.

A little old woman came to the half door. "Hello, yourself," she said, "and will ye come in now?"

"God bless all here," said Denny, as he stepped through the door.

"And ye too," said the old woman.

The tiny house was full of the good smell of burning peat. An old man sat by the fire, nodding at them in a friendly way. He was brown and wrinkled, with a fringe of white hair and a beard that jutted straight out from his chin.

"Mr. McManus, your honor, sorr," Denny began.

"No honor about it," broke in the old man, "to be Old McManus is honor enough. And what name would ye be having at all?"

"If you please, sorr, I'm Denny Foley, and this is David Trent that's come from America to visit his grandmother, Mrs. Hazlett at Slieverow House."

"I mind the Foleys," said the old man, "and I mind Mrs. Hazlett of Slieverow House."

Mrs. McManus was nodding her head. "Mrs. Hazlett was a Cascaden," she said, "and they were real quality. It would be your mother, now, that went off to foreign parts," she said to David.

"To America," said David.

"Miss Mary was the fine lass, and Miss Annie, her sister, is the dear wee thing," said Mrs. McManus, "and her going off to Alaska, I hear. Och, but that would be a perishing cold country, I'm thinking."

Old McManus was looking at the boys out of sharp blue eyes. "And what would ye be coming to see an

old man about? " he asked.

Denny flushed red and held up his two fists. " Would you look at them now," he said.

The old man nodded. " Covered with warts like a toad. And it's me ye want to cure them." He heaved himself out of his chair with a groan. " My rheumatism's that bad," he said. But he hobbled across the room to the ladder leading to the loft above, and with many more groans he climbed it and disappeared from sight. When he came down he had a piece of paper in his hand. They watched while he turned the corners in carefully. " Mind ye don't be opening it or be telling a living soul about it," he warned Denny. " Bury it beside the road, and the warts will leave ye."

" Thank you kindly," said Denny.

" And would ye be stopping for a mouthful of tea? " asked Mrs. McManus.

" No, thank you," said David. " My grandmother will be expecting me."

Old McManus seemed very well pleased with himself. " If ye meet a fairy in the wood," he said, " just turn your jackets inside out, and he'll not harm ye."

" But we haven't any jackets," said David. His answer seemed to please the old man, who went off into a wheezing chuckle that kept up until the boys were out of earshot.

" Are Mr. and Mrs. McManus the Little People? " asked David.

" Of course not," said Denny shortly, " but don't be talking about them here." They were walking through the wood at a fast clip, so that David had to watch where he was going. He didn't ask any more questions. But when they came out on the road Denny spoke again. " I told you not to talk about the Little People in there. Of course Old McManus isn't one of them. He's just good with the warts, but they say it's the wee folk that help him." Just then he saw a stick lying beside the road, and picking it up, he drove it into the ground two or three times until he had made a small hole. Then he put the folded paper in the hole and spread dirt over it. David saw that his hands were almost covered with warts. No wonder he wants to get rid of them! he thought.

" Do you really think that piece of paper will do any good? " he asked.

" I do," said Denny. " The warts are as good as gone this very minute."

" Maybe you'd better not tell your grandmother where we've been," said Denny after a while.

" Doesn't she like the McManuses? " asked David.

" She wouldn't believe that Old McManus has any power over warts at all. She doesn't hold with such things and she's very set in her ways."

David thought that over. " I won't tell," he decided. " But I like those people. I like the way they talk and I like their flower garden. Let's go see them again sometime."

Mrs. Hazlett was standing at the half door, watching for them. She smiled at Denny. " Did you lads have a good tramp? " she asked.

" Yes, fine," said David. He turned to Denny. " You'll come over again, won't you? "

" I will," said Denny, and went away whistling.

" Wash up now, dear," said Mrs. Hazlett. " Tea is ready."

Mary McInnelly was hurrying to the table, with a steaming plate of potatoes boiled in their jackets. They all sat down while Mrs. Hazlett asked the blessing, then Mary jumped up again. " Laws-a-day," she cried. " I forgot the skin plates."

" In Donegal, they eat the prateys, skins and all," said Robert. He laughed and everyone joined in. It was very pleasant sitting there in front of the glowing peat fire. David felt cheerful and happy now that he had a friend.

He wondered if Old McManus could really cure warts. It was something to watch for. There sure were queer things going on in Ireland.

4

A LETTER CAME FROM ANNIE, SAYING SHE HAD FOUND work in the post office, substituting while the regular employees went on holiday. She was well and happy, and asked if they would please forward any mail that came for her.

Mrs. Hazlett read the letter without comment, but she readdressed a letter that came from James Mackie in Alaska and asked Robert to mail it. David, watching, was reassured. Perhaps his grandmother had forgotten all about her quarrel with Annie.

To David she was all that was kind and loving. " To-morrow is market day," she said. " Would you like to go with Ownie Kern when he takes the butter to market? "

" Fine," said David.

" You'll have to be up with the birds," Ownie told him. " We must be up and away by five in the morning."

It was churning day, and when the breakfast work was cleared away, Mrs. Hazlett and Mary McInnelly went to the dairy. David followed them. The dairy was dim and quiet, with a stream of water running through t to keep it cool for the cream and butter. A dairy was lot nicer than an electric refrigerator, thought David, ut he couldn't imagine a stream of water running hrough their kitchen at home. On second thought, he had to decide in favor of the refrigerator.

Mrs. Hazlett skimmed the cream from the stone ars of milk that were ranged along the wall, and left Mary McInnelly to the churning. David watched until he pats of yellow butter, each stamped with a design of three wheat sheaves, stood in a row on the shelf.

" The wheat sheaves say that the butter was made at Slieverow House," said Mary. " Everyone at the market ooks for them. Your grandmother's butter is the best in the county, and it always brings a good price."

They were ready to leave the dairy when she turned back to pour some buttermilk into a dish that she set on the floor. " For the Little People," she said, " but don't tell your grandmother. She doesn't hold with them at all."

It seemed to David that he had just gone to bed when Ownie Kern called him. " Time to be off to market," said Ownie.

With eyes half shut he tumbled out of bed and hurried into his clothes. He was afraid of being late, but when he stepped out of the door into the yard, he found Ownie cutting the grass beside the ditch, and the donkey hitched to the two-wheeled cart was wandering down the road, nibbling grass as he went.

" I thought we were going to market," said David disappointed.

" We are," said Ownie. " I'm just after cutting

grass to pack the butter in. There's nothing finer to keep butter cool than grass cut fresh, with the morning's dew on it. Come, Wandering Billy," he shouted to the donkey, and at the call, the small donkey came obediently. Ownie packed the butter with the grass about it in a wicker creel and stowed it in the donkey cart. " Now for a bite of soda farl to stay the stomach and we'll be off," he finished and started for the kitchen.

They ate the soda farls as they rode along, and to David's mind nothing had ever tasted better. The sun was just up and the dew still sparkled on the green hedgerows. The air was filled with the singing of birds.

" Hark to the cuckoo now," said Ownie, " and the lark soaring into the blue sky."

Even Wandering Billy, the donkey, seemed full of the spirit of the morning as he trotted gaily down the road. A woman in the field sat on a three-legged stool, her red petticoats tucked up about her, and milked a cow. " The top of the morning to you," she called.

" And good luck to your work," said Ownie. " You must always give them the good word," he told David. " It would be a very bad sign if you didn't."

" Do you believe in signs? " asked David.

" And why not? " said Ownie. " Many's the time that listening to a sign would have saved a deal of trouble, I'm thinking."

They had reached the market town. Farm carts were drawn up on both sides of the road, and women with shawls over their heads were spreading out their goods for sale: vegetables and flowers, butter and eggs. There was a cartload of turf too, and some black calves were wandering about while a few men in stiff black hats

ooked them over. Suddenly, one of the men struck his
st into his open palm with a smack that sounded above
ll the din of the shouting and clattering crowd.

David was startled. " Is he going to start a fight? "
e asked.

" He's bought a calf," said Ownie, " and that sealed
he bargain."

Mary McInnelly had been right when she had said
hat the butter from Slieverow House was in great
demand. Ownie did a brisk business while David sat
lone in the cart. The sun was warm and he had been
ip a long time. He began to yawn.

" Och, for shame, to be gaping," said a voice at his
lbow, and there was Denny Foley, grinning beside
.im.

" How did you get here? " asked David.

" On my two feet. How else? " said Denny. " Michael
he Fiddler is down the road," he went on. " Come
way and hear him play."

The boys found a small crowd had gathered at a
tone bridge that crossed a small stream. They were
istening to a man sawing away at his fiddle. The music
et everyone's feet to tapping. Then a girl stepped out,
nd lifting her skirts, began to dance, her white stock-
ngs twinkling in and out beneath her red petticoats.
Vith a shout a man joined her, and they danced a
ig together. When it was over, Michael put his fiddle
inder his arm and passed the hat.

" I'm sorry," said David, embarrassed, " I haven't
ny money but an American dollar."

" That's all right," said a girl's voice. " I'll put in a
denny for you."

David turned gratefully to see a girl about his own

age. She had dark hair done in two thick braids and very blue eyes with black eyelashes. " I'm Lynn McClintock," she said. It was the girl he had seen riding horseback when he was with Robert.

" I'm David Trent," he said. " I'm visiting my grandmother."

" I know all about you," said Lynn. Her glance moved to Denny. " How are the warts? " she asked in a loud, clear voice.

When Denny turned brick red and hid his hands behind his back, she spoke severely. " I told you to go to Old McManus."

" I did," mumbled Denny.

" All right, then," said Lynn, mollified. " Sometimes it takes time, but Old McManus never fails."

" Do you believe that? " asked David.

She gave him a look. " And why not? " she asked.

David shrugged. She sure was a bossy character, he thought to himself.

The crowd was breaking up and they turned back with the others. Denny was looking somewhat anxiously from one to the other. " David went with me to see Old McManus," he said.

" I suppose you rode," said Lynn. " Americans never walk."

" What do you mean? " flared David. " Americans can walk just as far as you can, I'll have you know."

Lynn shrugged. " I ride mostly," she said.

David could think of nothing to say. He was glad to see Ownie coming to meet them.

" I've finished now," said Ownie. " We'll go for a bite of something at the Sullivan Arms."

David suddenly found that he was starving.

"I'll go with you," said Lynn. "I'm to meet my daddy there."

"Are you coming too?" David asked Denny. But Denny shook his head and turned away. "Would it be all right to ask him to eat with us?" David asked Ownie in an undertone.

"Your grandmother would never grudge it," said Ownie.

"Denny," shouted David, "come on and eat with us."

Denny wheeled joyfully. "Do you mean it, now?" he cried. "Many's the time I've passed by the Sullivan Arms, but never did I think to see the inside of it, much less to eat there."

When they entered the place, Mrs. Sullivan looked doubtfully at Denny. No Foley had ever had the price of a meal at the Sullivan Arms. But Ownie put her mind at rest. U. S. 1181823

"It's Mrs. Hazlett's grandson as wants Denny to eat with him," he explained.

"And I'm going to eat with them," said Lynn. "I shan't wait for my father. No knowing when he'll be along anyway."

Mrs. Sullivan's face cleared. The Hazletts and the McClintocks were good customers. She had nothing to worry about. She led the way to the dining room where one big table stood ready for all who came. A red-cheeked maid bobbed a curtsy, then stared at Denny.

"It's my cousin Rose," said Denny, beaming. "You didn't look to see the likes of me eating at the Sullivan Arms. Now, did you?" he asked her.

" Whist," warned Rose, looking anxiously at Mrs. Sullivan. " I haven't time to be gabbing with you now." And she hurried away to the kitchen to bring in the dinner.

" They have a lot of cabbage in Ireland," said David, looking at the serving dish she offered, where pale cabbage floated in a watery fluid.

" It's the time of year for cabbage," said Lynn, helping herself generously.

David never ate cabbage at home, but he didn't like to say so now. It wasn't a very good meal. The meat was stringy and the potatoes watery. But Lynn and Denny and Ownie were stowing it away with a will. David was hungry. Somewhat reluctantly he began to eat.

5

" Och, woman dear," a man's voice sounded in the lobby. " I declare you grow younger every year."

" Colonel McClintock, sir, how you talk," simpered Mrs. Sullivan as she followed a big, red-faced man into the dining room.

" Well, Lynn, lass," he said, " I see you didn't wait for me and a good thing too. And here is our Rose, blooming as ever, and Ownie and Denny." He gave a friendly nod to everyone.

" This is David Trent from America," said Lynn. " He's visiting his Grandmother Hazlett."

" A fine lady is Mrs. Hazlett," said the Colonel and gave David a clap on the back. With his coming into the dining room, Rose and Mrs. Sullivan were all eagerness to please. Mrs. Sullivan was fussing with the salt and pepper, the mustard and vinegar, and Rose ran giggling back and forth to fetch him the best of everything.

" Did Gillespie sell his heifer? " asked Lynn of her father.

" He did, and that's a fine beast, as fine, I'd say, as Mrs. Hazlett's Kerry cow. A rare beast is that one."

" But mean by nature," said Ownie. " Very free with her heels too."

" Is she now? " said the Colonel. " No telling about a cow. Give me a horse any time."

" Horses and dogs," said Lynn. " We have new puppies," she turned to the boys. " You must come and see them one day."

" Any more veg? " asked Rose, who was hovering about. She looked at Denny, who shook his head. " Sure now? " she urged. She brought the dessert then, a pale-colored gelatine so stiff David found it hard to cut with his spoon.

The Colonel looked at it and waved it away. " No cold shape for me, thank you. Just a bit of cheese, my dear, and a biscuit." He turned to Ownie. " Have you found anything new in the bog lately? " he asked.

" Nary a thing," said Ownie.

" The bog's a rare place to find things," the Colonel explained to David. " If nothing else, there may be some bog butter, put away by a housewife long ago to keep cool until market day and then lost or forgotten. Often it lies there for years, and sometimes it's good even then. Aye, the bog is a great place. I suppose you've seen your grandmother's ax? What wouldn't I give for that ax! " He sighed and pushed back his chair. " Well, lass, I must be off to Mr. Black's. Wait here for me." With a nod he left them.

" Now may the good Lord forgive your daddy for the sin of covetousness," said Ownie, looking after him.

Lynn laughed. " Daddy would be entranced to own that ax," she said, " but he's got his head full of a new plan. John Steenson of the Rock has given up at last and is going to live with his daughter in Newry, and Daddy is going to buy his place. He's gone to the solicitor's now to sign the papers."

" Has he now? " said Ownie. " And I suppose he'll be digging there for treasure."

" He will," said Lynn. She turned to David. " They call John Steenson ' John of the Rock' because there's a cromlech on his place."

" A cromlech? " repeated David.

" Yes, you know — those big stones that people set up ages ago, and nobody knows what they were for! There's a cairn too — a mound of dirt and stones — built by those same prehistoric people. Daddy's mad about prehistoric people and he's planning to dig in that mound. He expects to find something as good as your grandmother's ax buried in it."

" I wonder that he'd care to dig there," said Denny, who had been quiet during the meal, a bit awed by his surroundings. " He'll disturb the Little People, I'm thinking. It's well known that they meet at the cairn. John of the Rock never mowed the grass for fear of them."

" Denny Foley! " cried Lynn. " What foolishness are you talking? Think shame to yourself."

There she goes again, thought David, and spoke quickly to save his friend. " My mother told me about those stones. I'd like to see them."

" So you shall," said Lynn. " Don't you have them in America? "

" No," said David. " Only Indians lived there before Columbus, and they didn't leave much besides arrowheads."

" I know about Indians," said Lynn. " I've read *The Last of the Mohicans.*" She pronounced it with the accent on the first syllable.

" Mo-*hi*-cans," said David.

Lynn looked stubborn, then she smiled. " Well, I suppose you know because you live with them," she said.

" There aren't any Indians where I live," said David.

" There must be," said Lynn firmly.

David felt his temper rising. " There are not," he said hotly.

Lynn stared at him. " Hoighty-toighty," she said.

" Hoighty-toighty, yourself," David shouted right back to her.

The kitchen door opened, and Rose stuck her head around the corner, looking worried. " Any more cold shape? " she asked.

" No, thank you," said David, already ashamed of his outburst.

Lynn, too, was ready to drop the argument. " Probably where you live it's different," she conceded.

David shook his head, but he didn't say anything. What's the use? he said to himself. You can't win.

Denny was anxious to change the subject. " John of the Rock has a cousin by the same name," he said. " They call him Tidy John so as to tell them apart."

" Is it because he is tidy? " asked David, glad to switch to a safer topic.

" Aye, he's an old bachelor who lives all alone, and he washes his own corduroy pants so that they are always as neat as a pin."

" Tidy John," Ownie, who had sat silent during the

argument, took up the tale, " is the best slanesman in the county."

" A slanesman," Lynn explained quickly, " is a man who uses a slane to cut peat in the bog. Tidy John always works for your grandmother when they are turf-making. You'll see him one day."

" A hard man to get along with is Tidy John," said Ownie.

" They do say he's on good terms with no one but the powers of darkness," said Denny.

" There you go again," said Lynn. " Tidy John is a harmless old fellow. He wouldn't say boo to a goose, much less deal with the powers of darkness."

Anybody could see that Lynn was used to having her own way. No one said a word after she was through with this speech, but David could feel his temper rising again. Perhaps Ownie suspected this, for he stood up rather quickly.

" It's high time we were on our way home," he said. " Can we give you a lift, Denny? The butter creel is empty, and you can sit in it on the way home! " They all laughed at the thought of Denny sitting in the butter creel, and Denny's face was beaming.

" I'm just after eating at the Sullivan Arms, and now I'll be riding home in Mrs. Hazlett's donkey cart. This is a fine and happy day for Dennis Foley."

" I'll have to wait here for my father," said Lynn, following them to the lobby where Mrs. Sullivan sat knitting. She settled herself in one of the black leather chairs. " Now, David," she said, " Denny will fetch you over to Bride's Hill, and I'll show you the pups. Then we can go to John of the Rock's, and I'll show you the

41

cromlech and the cairn." She was looking at him almost as though she was afraid he might refuse.

"Well, thanks a lot," said David. But he had already made up his mind. He was going to stay away from Bride's Hill and this bossy character.

Wandering Billy, rested and refreshed with hay, seemed glad to head for home. Denny was so pleased with his day that he was good company, and they had a cheerful ride together.

"What did you mean about Tidy John and the powers of darkness?" asked David, who was curious to hear more now that they were safe from Lynn's interference.

But Ownie spoke quickly. "If your grandmother hears such talk as that, she'll be saying that Denny's no fit friend for you," he warned.

"You don't need to worry about that," said David. "I wouldn't say a word to her about it." But Ownie looked so disturbed that David thought best to talk of other things. Time enough to ask Denny when they were alone, he decided. "What kind of puppies does Lynn have?" he asked now.

"Irish terriers, they are," said Denny," as fine as they make them."

"We have a Boston bull. His name is Crackers," said David. And for the rest of the way home the talk was all of such safe things as dogs and the true elegance of the Sullivan Arms, the likes of which could not be found between here and Dublin, Denny declared. But in the back of his mind David was still curious. Tidy John and the powers of darkness were just another of those Irish tales, but just the same he wanted to hear more about them.

42

They dropped Denny off at his house and drove on. "It's been a nice day," David said to Ownie. "I'd like to go to market with you again."

"If your grandmother is willing," said Ownie. He cast an uneasy glance at David. "Bear in mind, my lad, that this talk of Little People and signs and the powers of darkness is not for your grandmother's ears. She doesn't hold with the like of that."

"I guess that Lynn doesn't hold with it either," said David. "If she isn't the bossy character! Who does she think she is anyway?"

"She's the only daughter of Colonel McClintock of Bride's Hill," said Ownie. "There's not a soul to say her nay, but you'll find her heart is in the right place for all that."

6

EVERYONE GOT UP EARLY AT SLIEVEROW HOUSE. ROB-
ert was the first one down after Mary McInnelly. When
David heard his step on the stair, he hurried out of bed
and into his clothes and followed him to the byre.
Ownie Kern sat on a low milking stool, his shoulder
pressed hard into the flank of the small Kerry cow while
a stream of rich milk flowed into the pail. His position
looked very uncomfortable.

" Why do you sit hunched over like that? " asked
David.

" Because this blackhearted little beast would kick
the milk pail over if I didn't," said Ownie. " She
knows she gives the best milk on the farm and she
suffers from the sin of pride. She's given to waiting
until the pail is full, then ups with her heels and kicks
it over. If I push my shoulder into her side, she can't
do that."

He had finished milking, and now he carefully
moved the pail out of harm's way before he stood up.
Quick as a flash the cow, who had stood patient and
quiet during the milking, lifted her hind foot in a kick.
But the pail was not there. " Ah ha! " said Ownie,

" you missed it," and he gave her a friendly slap before going on to the next cow.

When the milking was done they went back to the house for breakfast. A while later Denny turned in at the gate. " Lynn McClintock sent me over to fetch you," he said. " She wants to show you the pups."

" I don't think I want to go," said David, who was still irked by Lynn and her bossy ways.

" Och, now, of course you want to go," said his grandmother, who had overheard their talk. " Lynn is a good wee lass, and a lonesome one without a mother and only that Mrs. Guilaland to take care of her. You'll like it at Bride's Hill, with their fine horses and dogs," she finished.

" How far is it? " asked David.

" Not far," said Denny.

David looked at him suspiciously. " An Irish mile, I suppose," he said.

" It's only across the fields a bit," Denny assured him. He led the way across lots to a break in the hedge where steps led up and then down into the next field. David stopped to look at it. It was very neat and easy to climb.

" Say," he said, " that's really keen."

" What, the stile? " asked Denny in surprise. " Don't you have stiles in America? "

" Well, no," admitted David.

" What do you have then? "

" We just have barbed-wire fences," said David. " You crawl under them and snag your clothes while you're doing it. We don't go across lots much, I guess. But, Denny," he went on, " I want to ask you more about Tidy John and the powers of darkness. What — "

But Denny wasn't listening. " Look out! " he shouted, and started across the field at top speed.

" What's the matter? " asked David. But at the same moment he saw a bull charging straight at him. For a dreadful minute his legs refused to move. Then he, too, was tearing across the field. Denny was the first over the hedge and turned to drag David after him while the bull, pawing and snorting, came to a halt on the other side.

" Are — are there any more bulls around? " asked David.

" You're scared," said Denny.

" You ran as fast as I did," David defended himself.

" That was only to please the bull," said Denny. " He likes to think he can scare you." He made a face at the bull. " That's for you," he said and turned to go on.

They crossed another field, this one empty, and came to a gate that Denny opened and closed behind them. Some sheep were gazing quietly on a broad, green lawn. An avenue of trees led away to a great, square stone house with windows set in regular rows, each one topped by a carved stone ledge. Stone urns stood at either side of the great doorway. From a distance the house looked very fine, but when they came nearer, David could see that the urns were filled with weeds, and the steps leading to the front door were broken. Grass grew in the chinks of the wall. Everything looked run-down and uncared for.

" I expect Lynn is at the back," said Denny. He led the way around the house to the barns, which were as

46

well kept up as the house had been neglected. Sleek
horses looked out of their stalls, their coats shining. A
groom was exercising a nervous colt, who shied and
reared as the boys came into sight.

"Hup-hup, there's a pretty boy," soothed the groom.

"Good morrow, Tom Toolin," said Denny, slowing
down so as not to frighten the colt. They skirted the
yard, and coming to an empty stall, found Lynn playing with the puppies.

47

"It's all right, Bridie, dear," she reassured the mother dog, who was watching with a proud but anxious eye. "Aren't they darling wee things?" she asked, her voice gentle.

"They sure are cute," said David, watching the puppies tumbling over one another. "Have you named them yet?"

"I thought we'd do it today," said Lynn. "David can be the first to choose a name, because he's a guest." She picked up the biggest pup and held it lovingly. "What do you want to name this one?" she asked.

David was pleased. "Our dog at home is called Crackers," he said, "but you don't have crackers over here, only soda farls — "

"Farl, that's it," said Lynn. "Farl of Bride's Hill. It's an elegant name." She picked up a second pup, "Now, Denny, you can name this one."

"Sullivan Arms," said Denny without stopping to think for a minute. They were laughing when Colonel McClintock looked in at them.

"I'm going over to see John of the Rock," he said. "He's moving today. Do you want to come along?"

"We do," said Lynn. "I'll show David the cromlech and the cairn. The last puppy can wait for his name. There, Bridie," she said to the mother dog, "we'll leave you with your children."

As they stepped out into the courtyard, one of the horses nickered softly. "Och, Mayo, my darling," said Lynn, stroking his soft nose. "He's mine," she said to David. "Isn't he the beauty? That one is Sligo, Daddy's mount, and beyond is Monaghan, a good carriage horse. They're all named for the counties of Ireland,

48

you know. The colt is Wicklow Boy, and Daddy expects great things of him. Wait for us, Daddy," she called to the Colonel, who had started on ahead.

They were walking through a rutted lane between high banks when the Colonel stopped and pointed. " The cromlech," he said.

High above them, on the top of the bank, towered three great upright stones, with a fourth across the top like a gigantic table. Covered with moss, they looked immensely old as though they had stood there since time began.

" Boy! " said David. " However did they get there? "

" Other people have wondered about that," said the Colonel. " Probably the stones were levered into place by propping hardwood logs under them. Then the top stone was let down from above. Those ancient men were skilled workmen, and they must have used some kind of organization to be able to build such monuments as this. Come now, and I'll show you the cairn."

They climbed the bank, passed the cromlech, which, close up, seemed even bigger, and came to a well-kept field. But strangely enough, in the middle was a low mound, unkempt and overgrown with whins, while on the top grew a young thorn tree.

" It's the cairn," said the Colonel proudly. " You can see it's man-made by the circle of stones around it." He pointed, and sure enough in the undergrowth, big stones, some fallen or broken, others half-covered with weeds and earth, ringed the mound. " They were put there to keep the cairn from falling away," explained the Colonel.

David remembered his mother's story. " Is there a

crock of gold in there? " he asked.

The Colonel shook his head. " No," he said, smiling. " The cairn is probably a chieftain's grave. The cromlech also may mark a grave, or it may have been a place of worship. People used to think that the druids, the ancient priests of Ireland, built these things, but we know better now. They're thousands of years older than that, built by seafaring folk who came from Spain and Portugal long before the Phoenicians or the Greeks began their trading. They were looking for Ireland's copper and gold, and they brought the idea of these monuments with them. There are hundreds of cairns and cromlechs in Ireland, you know." His eyes flashed with enthusiasm, then he smiled. " That's enough of a lecture for one day," he said. " We must go to see old John Steenson. You understand now," he turned to David, " why we call him John of the Rock."

Just beyond a thicket they came to John Steenson's cottage. The old man sat in a rocker in the yard, his furniture stacked around him while his daughter supervised its loading onto her husband's cart.

" Well, John," said the Colonel, " it's a good day for the flitting. May you have many more of them."

" Thanking you kindly," said John Steenson in a doleful voice, " it's not likely at all that I will be lasting many days, uprooted as I am."

" Och, don't talk that way," said the Colonel. " Remember, now, when you were laid up last winter with no one to take care of you. You'll be better off with your daughter in Newry."

But the old man shook his head. " I'd never be going if it wasn't that my black cat, Satan, up and died on me. 'Twas a sign."

" Poor Satan," Lynn sympathized, " and a fine, handsome beast he was too."

John of the Rock gave her an approving glance. " 'Tis a good lass," he said.

" I've brought you a bit of a present," said the Colonel. " 'Tis the shawl that was my father's favorite." With that he tucked a plaid blanket over the old man's knees.

John of the Rock permitted himself a smile. " A fine man was your father, and pleased I am to have his shawl," he said.

His daughter came out of the house with a cup of tea for her father. " The kettle's on the boil," she said to the Colonel. " Can I give you a cup? "

" No, thanks," he said. " We've just had a look at the cairn. It will be a grand sight when the weeds are cleared away."

John of the Rock sat up with a jerk and banged his cane on the ground. " I forbid it," he shouted.

" Now, Father, don't excite yourself," soothed his daughter. But the old man was taken with such a fit of coughing that he couldn't speak.

" Man alive, what ails you? " cried the Colonel, thumping him on the back while his daughter seized the cup to keep it from spilling.

When John of the Rock had at last regained his breath, Lynn spoke softly. " Man dear, why don't you want the weeds cleared away? "

" That land has belonged to the Little People since the memory of man," said John of the Rock. " Many's the time I've wished I could plant it. But, no, I wouldn't clear it. If you disturb it, I warn you now, you'll bring bad luck on the entire world. I'm speaking no lie."

After that he buried his face in his teacup, which his daughter had returned to him. For a minute no one spoke.

"It's cold and damp out there on the cairn," said Lynn at last. "The Little People would be far from comfortable. Why shouldn't they meet in your cottage instead, now that you're leaving it? Daddy would let them. Wouldn't you, Daddy?"

The Colonel's face was red, and he had to swallow several times, but at last he brought himself to nod his head. John of the Rock was satisfied.

"Aye," he said, "no doubt they'd like that." The furniture was by this time all stacked on the cart, and the old man's daughter brought the key to the cottage.

"Where will you be keeping the key?" demanded John of the Rock.

"Under the leek bush beside the door," said Lynn quickly before her father could speak. "It will be right handy for the Little Folk."

"Aye, a good place," said the old man.

"Now, Father," said his daughter, "we'll just be putting your chair on the cart, and with the shawl over your knees you'll be as snug as in front of your own turf fire."

"Heave ho," said the Colonel, and he and the old man's son-in-law lifted John of the Rock, chair and all, onto the cart. "God be with you," said the Colonel.

"And all here," said John of the Rock. They rode away without looking back.

7

"I can't find a living soul willing to work at the cairn," said Colonel McClintock, "though I have permission from the Government to dig there."

"What's the matter with them?" asked Lynn.

"They're afraid of the Little People. In my entire life I have never heard of such nonsense."

David and Lynn, who had been playing with the puppies, sat back on their heels and stared at him. "Did you tell them you were going to give John Steenson's cottage to the fairies in place of the cairn?" asked Lynn.

"I did not," snorted the Colonel. "I'll not be a party to such foolishness. What's the world coming to?"

"Well," said Lynn, "if no one else will do the work, you'll have to yourself."

Her father stopped his pacing. "I?" he said in a tone of surprise. "I never used a scythe in my life and I wouldn't be much better with a spade."

"Anybody can clear away weeds," said Lynn. "David and I will help. Denny too."

"Not Denny," said the Colonel. "It was Denny's father that was sitting with his feet up when I called

53

on him, and he actually had the face to say he was too busy. ' You're thinking of the Little People,' I said. ' I am,' said he. And that was the end of it.''

Lynn got to her feet, the light of determination in her eye. " If you can't find anyone to clear the cairn, we'd better get at it ourselves. What will we be needing to take with us? "

" Well," said her father uncertainly, " a scythe, I suppose — "

" And a spade," said Lynn, " and a sickle to cut the short grass, and a broom. That will be enough to start with. Come on, David, we'll get them."

" Well — " said her father again. But there was no stopping Lynn. Armed with an assortment of tools, they were soon on their way to the cairn. The Colonel was chuckling. " If you want a thing well done," he said, " do it yourself."

They climbed the bank by the cromlech and crossed the plowed field to the cairn. " Keep your distance now," warned the Colonel as he began to swing the scythe. " I don't want to do anyone a mischief with this thing."

" I'll cut the short grass on the other side of the cairn," said Lynn, waving the sickle, " and David, you can clear away the dirt on the stones that have fallen down."

Bossy as ever, thought David, but he set to work on the stones without saying anything. Lynn squatted down on the edge of the cairn, chopping away at the short grass with the sickle, and the Colonel, grunting a little, wielded the scythe. It was a lovely day. Bees hummed in the clover, and the scent of newly cut grass rose on the air.

54

" Here comes Denny," cried Lynn, looking up from her work. " Now then, Denny, you take the sickle and get to work, and I'll go over and inspect what Daddy's doing." She thrust the sickle at Denny as she spoke. But he backed away, the red coming up into his face, then ebbing to leave his freckles dark against his skin.

" What's the matter? " asked Lynn. " You're not afraid of the Little People too."

" I am not," said Denny, his pride touched.

" You don't need to be," said Lynn. " Daddy has said they can meet in John Steenson's house. It's much better than out in the damp and the cold. The key is under the leek bush, though of course," she added, " we don't hold with such nonsense."

Sickle in hand, Denny marched to a place beyond David. There he knelt down and seized a handful of grass; then, with the sickle upraised, he began to speak in a soft monotone. " Your honors," he mumbled, " you'll find the key to the wee cottage under the leek bush. Make yourselves at home. 'Tis much better for you to meet under a roof than out here in the damp and the cold. Under the leek bush, mind, is where you'll find the key."

David listened with a queer feeling down his spine. Was Denny really talking to the fairies? He glanced at Lynn and her father, but they didn't seem to have heard. Denny had gone to work with the sickle, and David went back to give a final sweep, then cried out in surprise. " There's some sort of picture on here," he said.

The Colonel came running to stare at a design of swirling curves that covered the whole face of the stone. " Spirals," he said. " They're often found on these old stones. They were probably some kind of magic signs. Good work, David lad! " He seized the broom and swept some more. When the design showed clearly enough, he fumbled in his pocket and brought out an old envelope and a pencil. " I'll just make a sketch of it and take it home to compare with the books," he said.

" Daddy knows all about such things," said Lynn proudly. " He studied in Dublin at the university."

The picture finished, the Colonel stooped to pick up the scythe, which had fallen to the ground, then clapped his hand to his back with a groan. " Och! " he cried. " Whatever have I done to my poor back now? "

" You'll be all right," soothed Lynn. " It's just a wee crick. What you need," she added on an inspiration, " is your tea."

" I do," said her father, flexing his muscles carefully. " A twinge was all, I hope. Come away, then, all of you, and we'll have tea at Bride's Hill."

But when they reached the big house, Denny hung back. " Mother will be looking for me," he said.

Lynn laughed. " Since when did your mother look for you? " she asked. " Come away now to your tea, and no nonsense at all."

" We're pretty dirty," said David.

" You can wash in the scullery," Lynn told them.

After they had cleaned up, they had tea in the Colonel's study, a cheerful, shabby room where even Denny felt at home. Bridie had left her puppies in the stable and was curled up in the best chair, but she gave up her place to the Colonel, who lowered himself carefully into his seat. Mrs. Guilaland, the housekeeper, came in with a pot of tea and a plate of paper-thin bread and butter. " Woman dear," said the Colonel at the sight of it, " this is no food for famished laborers. It will disappear like snow out of a ditch. We need something to stick to the ribs."

Smiling a little, Mrs. Guilaland went away to come back with soda farls and cheese and great slabs of currant cake. When they had eaten it all, the Colonel took down a book from the shelf and turned the pages. " This tells about ancient Irish monuments," he said. " Here it is, the very spiral we found on the stone."

" It is," said Lynn, and passed the book on to the boys, then she gave a squeal. " Denny, your warts are gone! "

Denny was beaming. " I was after thinking it was time you noticed it."

" Daddy," shrieked Lynn, " Old McManus has charmed Denny's warts away."

" Has he now," said the Colonel, looking over his glasses. " Old McManus has a great name as a wart charmer, whether he deserves it or not. Warts are queer things. They come and they go, and no one knows why."

It was time for the boys to go home. " Come over first thing tomorrow," said Lynn, " so we can start work early."

" Not tomorrow," said her father, a hand on his back. " I need a day of rest if I'm not to be crippled entirely."

" But, Daddy, we can work by ourselves," said Lynn.

" No, I want to watch everything that is done," said the Colonel. " Too often ignorant workers do more harm than good. There must be no mistakes on this dig."

Lynn looked stubborn, but for once her father stood

firm. There was to be no work at the cairn without him. The Colonel took his day of rest, and then there was a spell of wet, rainy weather. It was several days before Denny brought the news that the Colonel was ready for work again. The boys found Lynn waiting impatiently.

" I've a wee besom here," she said. " It will be good for dusting the stones." She held a whisk broom made of twigs. " Smell," she ordered David and thrust it under his nose. A faint perfume came from it. " Heather," she said. " Cooper McPhilips makes the best besoms in the county."

The Colonel took charge when they got to the cairn. Denny was to use the sickle, David the spade, and Lynn would dust the stones with the besom, while the Colonel himself still wielded the scythe. They worked for a while in silence, then Lynn called out, " Another picture! "

The Colonel studied it. " 'Tis a boat," he decided.

" It doesn't look like a boat," Lynn objected.

" It's a boat all right," said her father. " What did I tell you? " he cried happily. " The men who built this cairn were seafarers. Och, we are the lucky beings to have found it. And we've done well with the work," he added as he looked proudly at what they had accomplished. The grass was mowed; several of the encircling stones stood clear and free of dirt and weeds. Only the thorn tree still stood on the top of the mound. " That is the thing to tackle next," he decided.

They all fell to work at it, the Colonel digging with the shovel and the others carrying off the loose stones that seemed to form the basis of the cairn. When the roots were well exposed, everyone laid hold of the

trunk and pulled under the direction of the Colonel. At first the roots held firm, then gave way with such a rush that Lynn lost her balance and sat down hard, and her father clapped a hand to his back with a groan. The tree lay on its side, the roots still quivering, when Denny's eye caught a glint of yellow. He reached out a hand and pried loose a pretty pebble that was caught in a lump of dirt between the roots.

" What is it? " asked Lynn.

But her father stretched out a hand that trembled. " Amber! " he cried, " amber, as I'm alive." Forgetting his back in his excitement, he took the pebble and

59

rubbed it against his sleeve; then, reaching into his pocket, he brought out a piece of paper and tore it into bits. Slowly he passed the pebble over the scraps of paper and they stirred, rising to meet it. " See, it's electrified," he said, his broad, red face redder than ever, his eyes glistening with excitement.

" But what is it? " asked Lynn again.

" You know what amber is," said her father. " They make beads of it, and pipestems. It's fossilized resin from pine trees. In ancient times people thought it had magic because it generates electricity when rubbed, and of course no one knew about electricity then. It was very precious and was traded all over the known world. Only great men ever owned it, and it was buried in the graves of chieftains. To think that we have found a bead of amber! I can scarcely believe it."

His enthusiasm was catching. They passed the bead from hand to hand, laughing excitedly. " Here, Denny," said Lynn, " you're the one who found it. You can rub first." They took turns rubbing, and each time the bits of paper stirred obligingly. Then they got down on their knees to grub in the dirt, looking for another pebble. They examined the tree roots and poked about in the hole where the tree had stood; but at last they gave up the search, and the Colonel tied the one amber bead in his handkerchief.

" It's time to go home and record our find," he said. " The difference between a professional and an amateur job is a good deal in the way a dig is recorded. A professional puts down everything: dates, finds — but amateurs muddle through."

" We're professionals," said Lynn, " the Bride's Hill Antiquarian Society."

" Later we'll make some rubbings of the decorated stones," said the Colonel.

" What's a rubbing? " asked Lynn.

" A rubbing," explained her father, " is an exact copy of a design. You take strong paper and dampen it, then smooth it onto the design, tamping it down until every part is covered. Then you go over it all with a pad of ink — some people use shoe blacking — being sure to rub the ink in thoroughly. When it's dry you have a perfect copy, provided the work has been properly done."

" Put down in the record that David found the spirals and Denny the amber," said Lynn. " I found the boat, though I don't think it looks like one. When we dig in the mound, I'm sure I'll find something better."

" I have to go to Dublin tomorrow for a few days," said the Colonel regretfully. " Things will have to wait until I get back. I'll look in at the museum while I'm there. There's sure to be pottery in the cairn, and I'll brush up on how to restore it."

" Take me with you," begged Lynn. " I was the one who started the Antiquarian Society. I ought to go."

Her father hesitated, but Lynn was used to having her own way. "You'll have to be by yourself while I'm doing business," he said.

" I'll stay at the museum," said Lynn. " Please, Daddy."

" Well — " said her father.

Lynn went farther. " David and Denny worked too," she said. " They deserve to go to Dublin with us."

Her father laughed. " Not so fast," he said. " The lads deserve it all right, but I can't take everyone to

61

Dublin, you know. I'll tell you what, though," he went on, " we'll plan an outing for later. What do you say to that? "

" I'd like it fine," said Denny.

" So would I," said David.

Lynn was rubbing the amber bead again. " It's pretty," she said. She put a pin on the floor and held the bead over it. The pin stirred, its point rising ever so little.

" It's magic," she said.

" Aye," said her father. " Magic three thousand years old."

8

" Now that the hay is in, it is a good time to cut more turf for the winter," said Mrs. Hazlett one morning at breakfast. " You'd better see when Tidy John can give you a hand in the peat bog."

Robert nodded. Whatever his mother suggested was always done, so very soon Tidy John came to work in the bog. David had not forgotten Denny's talk about Tidy John's dealings with the powers of darkness. Of course, he told himself, he didn't believe a word of it, but he couldn't help staring at the man who came into the yard with a slane over his shoulder. The slane looked like a narrow spade with an extra piece of metal that stood at right angles to it. Robert had told him that with a slane a man could cut two sides of a brick of turf at the same time, which made the work go much faster. As far as David could see, Tidy John looked like most of the old men he had seen in Ireland. He had a brown, wrinkled face and a beard that encircled his chin, but his corduroy pants were very clean, and he looked so neat that Tidy John was a good name for him.

Robert and Ownie Kern got their slanes, and the

three men started off for the bog with David tagging along, for if anything was going to be found in the bog, he wanted to be there to see it.

Tidy John was a great worker, cutting the turf into neat, even bricks something like brown loaves of bread. The others worked steadily, but even David could see that Tidy John outdid them. The dark walls of peat left from the cutting rose from pools of black oily water. David watched eagerly. He would dearly love to be able to tell Lynn he had seen an ax or something in the bog. But all he saw were a few branches and twigs in the peat wall. They were bits of trees that had been buried in the moss, Robert told him.

"They make the finest kind of kindling in the world," he said, pulling out the branches and setting them to one side to dry. "You can help with the work if you like. Stack the peat bricks on end so the air can circulate through to dry them."

They were oozing with oily water. "Will they ever dry?" asked David.

"The wind and sun will do it," said Ownie, who had laid down his slane to stack the turf.

"It's a lot of work," said David. "At home we have an oil burner. All we have to do is telephone when we want more oil, and the truck brings it."

"That's America for you," said Ownie. "Now, we have to work for our fuel. When the turf is dry it has to be cocked into a rick beside the house and then thatched with straw to keep out the rain."

There was little talking during the morning. Tidy John tended strictly to business, and the others sweated trying to keep up with him. It was only at lunch, which

64

Mary McInnelly brought at noon, that Ownie and Tidy John fell to talking. " Have ye heard about the ghost that's been seen at the Dark Angle? " asked Tidy John. " A figure all in white has been seen walking back and forth and groaning the while."

" What nonsense! " said Robert.

" The schoolmaster saw it," said Tidy John. " He struck at it with his blackthorn stick, and it floated away over the hedge in the shape of a folded handkerchief."

" With the ghost inside the handkerchief, I make no doubt," scoffed Robert.

Tidy John thrust out his chin so that his beard stuck out straight in front of him. " Would you be calling me a liar then? " he demanded.

But Robert stood his ground. " I'll say it again, it's nothing but foolish chatter."

" And now he's after calling me a fool," said Tidy John, jumping to his feet. " I'll just be taking myself off, and it's yourself that can be finishing the turf-making."

Through all this, Ownie had been trying to catch Robert's eye, making signs and shaking his head. But Robert refused to look his way. " Suit yourself," he said to Tidy John, and the old man shouldered his slane and marched away.

" Now why did you pick a fight with Tidy John? " Ownie burst out. " You know in your heart and soul 'tis best to keep on the good side of him."

" Och," said Robert, " the blatherskite! Good riddance to him. Come now, we've no time to waste. There's work to be done."

But now all the happiness of the day was gone. They worked in glum silence, Ownie disapproving, Robert surly. When it was time to lay off work, Robert started for home without a word, leaving David to follow with Ownie. David looked at the dark, oily bricks of turf neatly stacked to dry. " Even without Tidy John there's enough peat for the winter, isn't there? " he ventured.

" It shrinks when it's dry," said Ownie, " and likely as not," he added gloomily, " Tidy John will have put a spell on it so what we have won't burn at all."

David didn't say anything. Of course you couldn't argue with a grownup, but he didn't believe a word of it. How could any little old man put a spell on a load of peat?

" Now don't be telling your grandmother about this," warned Ownie as they started back. At the house he turned off to do the milking, and David went in to find the women busy preparing the evening meal. When everything was ready, his grandmother sent David out to call the men. They were standing together, their faces grave.

" I tell you she's dry," said Ownie.

" It can't be," said Robert.

" It is! Not a drop of milk did the Kerry cow give."

" But what ails her? " cried Robert.

" You may well ask, you that shamed Tidy John to his face," said Ownie severely. " It's himself as has bewitched the poor beast. Not a doubt of it."

David had come up in time to overhear their conversation. They turned to look at him with unsmiling faces. " Not a word to your grandmother," was all that Robert said to him.

" I won't tell," said David.

Robert turned back to Ownie. " They'll be churning in another day," he said. " She'll know then. Without the Kerry cow's milk there won't be much of a churning. You'll have to help me, Ownie. We've worked together this long time. You can't desert me now."

Ownie was silent, staring at the ground for so long that David grew anxious. Then he spoke slowly. " I'll do what I can," he said. " 'Tis the dark of the moon. We must bring the cows up from pasture and shut them in the byre. When your mother is asleep in her bed, meet me in the kitchen. I'll do my best."

Robert drew a deep breath. " More power to you," he said.

He turned then and started for the house, but David pulled at his uncle's sleeve. " I want to come too. Please, please," he said.

" Can you keep your mouth shut? " asked Robert.

" Oh, I can, Scout's honor."

" David," said his grandmother as they sat at the table, " you look flushed. Do you feel all right? "

" I feel fine," said David, and hastily stuffed a whole scone into his mouth so that he couldn't answer any more questions.

" Did the lad work too hard at the turf-making? " asked Mrs. Hazlett, turning to Robert.

" He's all right. Look at the color in his cheeks," said Robert.

" Yes," agreed his mother, " the skim-milk look is gone. But he had better go to bed early, and you too, Robert. You don't look yourself."

Robert laughed it off, but he mounted the stairs soon after his mother went to bed. The kitchen was very quiet. David lay with his eyes wide open, staring at the fire. It was banked for the night, but once in a while a bit of peat would flare up for a minute and then die down again. He was determined not to sleep, but he had had a long day in the open air. In spite of himself, he drifted off and then woke with a start at the sound of something falling. People were moving about in the dark room.

" Dropping your boot on the floor," came Ownie's angry whisper. " Is it that you want to wake your mother at all? "

" It slipped from my hand," said Robert.

David was out of bed and pulling on his sweater. He could just make out Ownie standing by the fireplace. Somehow Ownie seemed taller than life and very commanding, quite different from his usual easygoing self.

" What do you want me to do? " asked Robert humbly.

" First," said Ownie, " the lad here will go to the parlor and get the tongs that are beside the hearth."

" Me? " cried David. The parlor was a room set apart. No one went in there except on special occasions. David had stood in the doorway one time, watching while his grandmother and Mary McInnelly had given the room a cleaning. Afterward the door was shut and not opened again until it was time for the next cleaning. He didn't feel like going into that strange room all by himself in the middle of the night. " I don't think my grandmother would want me to," he said.

" Och, but she won't know," said Ownie.

68

"But why do I have to go to the parlor for tongs?" asked David. "There are tongs right here in the kitchen."

Ownie sighed impatiently. "If anything went wrong with the kitchen tongs, they'd know about it in a moment of time. But the parlor tongs now, no one would notice them for a while."

"But if anything went wrong —" repeated David, his voice trembling a little.

"It won't," said Ownie.

David wanted to say, "Why don't you get your own tongs?" but something about this new Ownie made him swallow the question. Very slowly he started down the dark passage to the parlor door. Just as he lifted the latch, a chunk of turf in the kitchen behind him split open and the fire blazed up. He pushed open the door. By the light of the fire he could see the grandfather clock in the corner and the shining brass tongs beside the fireplace. He crossed the room and had the tongs in his hand when the clock gave a loud whir and began to strike. It was too much. Forgetting everything in his panic, he raced back to the kitchen.

"Whist!" whispered Ownie. "Do you want to be waking your grandmother?" Taking the tongs from David, he stood listening, but nothing stirred. "Come," he said at last and stepped out of the door into the night. It was dark as pitch. David could see nothing at all. "Go to the byre and wait there," said Ownie and melted into the darkness.

David was holding tight to Robert. "Where has he gone?" he whispered.

"How should I know?" said Robert. He started

down the path to the byre, David clinging to him. It seemed, if anything, darker in the byre, but Robert was able to find his way around. He lighted a lantern and hung it on a nail. In the faint glow they could see the cows sleeping peacefully in their stalls, but the place seemed queer and unfamiliar.

" I don't think I like it much," said David. " Where has Ownie gone? "

" Stop your blathering," said Robert crossly, and fell to biting his nails.

" I don't like it a bit," said David again. " I wish I were home." Robert did not answer. They sat for a long time saying nothing at all.

9

DAVID STARED OFF INTO THE SHADOWS WITHOUT EVEN blinking. He couldn't have said what made him so scared. But scared he was. Robert was scowling and biting his nails. He wasn't any comfort at all. Then suddenly Ownie was there, breathing hard as though he had been running. He had the parlor tongs in his hand, and a wisp of straw was dangling from them.

" It's a bit of the thatch from Tidy John's roof," he said. " Now, Robert, fetch me a bucket."

David stared in surprise. This wasn't the way Ownie usually talked. But Robert went meekly to get the bucket. Ownie put the straw in it and put a match to the straw, which was wet with dew, and the match went out. He had to light one after another before a spark showed in the thatch. Then he blew on the spark and stirred the straw around with the tongs until at last it began to burn, but not with a good blaze. It smouldered and smudged, so that they were all soon coughing.

" There," said Ownie, straightening up at last. " Now offer the bucket to Minnie."

" Minnie? " said Robert, looking at the cow Minnie

71

sleeping peacefully in her stall. " There's nothing the matter with Minnie."

Ownie's eyes flashed in the light of the lantern. " Give it to Minnie," he ordered.

" Och, all right then," said Robert crossly. He pushed the smoking bucket under poor Minnie's nose, who, wakened from her sleep, lurched to her feet with an angry snort.

" Good," said Ownie, never minding at all how poor Minnie might feel. " Now," his voice rang out loud and clear, " give it to her that is bewitched."

The little Kerry cow was awake, and when Robert offered her the bucket, she stretched out her neck and nuzzled in the smoking thatch. Ownie gave a great sigh. " 'Tis a good night's work," he said. " Now we can be off to our beds."

David slept late the next morning. By the time he was awake, the men had breakfasted and left for the peat bog. Eating by himself, he thought back over last night's doings and almost hoped the whole thing had been a dream. He didn't feel happy about it.

His grandmother was watching him. " Davy," she said, " I think you had better stop home with me today. I'm afraid you have been overdoing."

" I'm fine," said David. " I like it at the peat bog and I can help some too. Besides, maybe we'll find another ax or something. I want to be there to see it."

His grandmother smiled. He had guessed right — nothing would please her better than for her grandson to be interested in the bog. " Be sure to come home if you get tired," she said.

Mary McInnelly was coming from the scullery with the broom and duster. " 'Tis the day for cleaning the parlor," she told David.

At the words, David's heart gave a lurch. The tongs, he thought, I forgot to put back the tongs. He crept quietly to the parlor door and looked in. The tongs were in their place, but he caught his breath at the sight of them. They were black with soot. Beside the shining andirons they stood out in horrid contrast.

" Mary McInnelly! " cried Mrs. Hazlett, " would you look at the fire tongs. Never in my life have I laid eyes on such a sight."

" Laws-a-day," said Mary, clucking in bewilderment. " And how could that be at all when there's been no fire in here since Easter? " She scurried away to get the brass polish, and David, not waiting to hear any more, let himself quietly out of the house.

He found Robert and Ownie cutting turf. " The top of the morning to you," said Ownie, who was very gay this morning.

" Good luck to your work," said David.

" That's the fine Irish lad for you," said Ownie. Robert said nothing. Indeed, he scarcely looked up from his work. David waited, hoping for news of the Kerry cow, but not a word was said about it. At last he could bear it no longer.

" Is the little Kerry cow all right? " he burst out. " Did she give milk this morning? "

When Robert did not answer, Ownie leaned importantly on his slane. " She did," he said. " Tidy John's spell is broken. He can do her no harm now." He was ready to go on talking about it, but Robert looked so

74

glum that David did not dare ask further, and even Ownie, after one glance, went back to the turf-making. David began stacking the bricks of peat, still hoping for news, but the morning wore away with everyone working almost in silence. It was a relief when Mary McInnelly came at noon with the lunch. She had a blanket over her arm.

"Your grandmother said you were to lie down for a nap," she told David. "You can spread the shawl on the grass in the shade of the hedge."

"Thank you," said David politely. "Are you going to stay to eat with us?" He was hoping she would say yes; maybe things would be pleasanter.

But she shook her head. "I have to get back," she said. But she stood around for a while wanting to talk. "A queer thing," she said, "when we were cleaning the parlor this morning — there were the fire tongs as black as your heel, and never a fire in the parlor since Easter, and me cleaning them every week of my life besides!" She looked from one to the other, but no one said anything.

David felt his face stiffen and spoke quickly. "It will be nice to lie down out here," he said, stammering a little. "Thanks a lot for the blanket."

"You're welcome," said Mary. She waited a moment, then, shaking her head, she turned toward home.

"She'll have the story out of us yet," said Ownie, watching her go.

"Not out of me," said Robert.

"I won't tell either," said David quickly.

After they had eaten, Robert spread the blanket in the shade. "Well, lad," he said, "you have it soft. Get your forty winks. I wish I could too."

It was pleasant lying there listening to the birds in the hedgerow. The rhythmic sound of the slanes and the splash of the water in the bog made a cheerful accompaniment.

Robert was bending over him. "Time to be going home," he said.

David started up. A great pile of turf had been cut and stacked while he slept. "I'm afraid I wasn't much help," he said ruefully. Ownie had gone on ahead. Robert helped roll up the blanket, and they started off together. "I guess you don't feel so good," ventured David as he looked at Robert's downcast face.

"I do not," said Robert. "The whole thing is past reason. For my entire life I've said these tales of spells and bewitchment were nonsense. And now look what's happened. Last night makes me out a liar. It's a terrible thing."

"You're no liar," said David.

"What do you mean?" asked Robert, looking hopeful.

David hadn't really meant anything except that he wanted to sympathize, but he blundered on. "I don't believe in spells," he said.

"No more do I," Robert burst out. "But the cow did go dry —"

They were crossing the pasture where the cows stood near the gate, waiting patiently to be milked. Almost at the same moment they both saw the overturned bucket beside the hedge. Robert had reached it in two strides. There was some milk still in the pail, and more was spilled on the grass around it.

76

" That Tidy John! " cried Robert. " The skellum milked the Kerry cow himself while we were cutting turf and hoped we'd believe he had bewitched her. But he didn't know the ways of the little beast," he laughed. " She waited until the pail was full and then she kicked it over. Och, she got the best of him."

" And she wasn't bewitched at all," said David.

" She was not, and if I hadn't been bewitched myself, I'd never have believed it. What a fool I've been," he cried, striking his forehead. " I'll be the laughingstock of the entire world."

" If we don't tell, no one will know," said David.

Robert stared at him. " Could you keep a secret? " he asked.

" Of course I could," said David.

Robert's face brightened and he thrust out a hand. " Shake on it," he said. " There's Ownie, of course," he went on after a minute.

" He's awfully proud of himself," David pointed out.

" He is that," Robert agreed, " but we'll have to chance his telling about it. If the story gets out, it will be another Irish tale. And if I ever get a bit beyond myself, I'll remember Tidy John and come down to earth." He laughed suddenly. " Davy," he said, " you're a broth of a boy."

All through the evening meal Robert was in gay spirits.

" Did you find a treasure in the bog that you're so happy? " asked his mother.

" It's David that finds treasures, amber and the like, for Colonel McClintock."

" I didn't find it really. It was Denny," said David.

77

" But when the Colonel comes back from Dublin, we're going to dig in the cairn and maybe there will be treasure."

" It's a bad thing to go digging there," said Ownie.

" The treasure might be fairy gold that would melt away when you touch it," said Mary McInnelly.

" Worse than that," said Ownie, shaking his head.

" If the Colonel finds anything at all, he'll be a happy man," said Robert.

" If he doesn't bring trouble on the lot of us with his digging," said Ownie gloomily. He was all against it.

When they rose from the table, Robert looked at David. " This lad should have a chance to roast some chestnuts in the fire," he said. " There's still a bag left in the shed." He brought in the bag and showed David how to range the chestnuts in front of the fire. " When they burst open they're done," he said, " but it's another matter to get them out of the fire. You can use the tongs to pull them out. You're a good lad with the tongs," he added, giving David a wink.

David glanced quickly at his grandmother. But she was smiling. " Many's the night we've roasted chestnuts," she said, " and Annie was always the one to get the chestnuts out of the fire for all of us."

10

DAVID SAT IN THE KITCHEN, WRITING A LETTER HOME. It was raining. It rained a great deal, though nobody seemed to mind. And it was cold. A blast of damp, chilly air blew through the open half door, and David drew his chair closer to the peat fire that smouldered in the great fireplace.

" Dear Mom and Dad," he wrote, " I'm having a fine time." He was too, he thought, and grinned a little sheepishly remembering what a fuss he had made about coming. " We found an amber bead in the cairn at John of the Rock's place," he went on. " Lynn and her dad have gone to Dublin, but when they come back, we're going to dig there for treasure." He stopped, trying to think what more to write about. He couldn't tell about the Kerry cow. That was a secret. Mom had sent him over to help Annie go to Alaska, but that was out. " I'm sorry I can't do anything about Annie," he wrote. " She isn't here. She's gone to Armagh."

His grandmother came into the room. " When is Annie coming home? " he asked.

" I don't know," said his grandmother. David sighed. It was always like that. She wouldn't talk about Annie.

" I like her," he said suddenly.

" Of course," said his grandmother. She took up the tongs and poked the fire into a blaze. " Why don't you write her a letter now? "

David had not counted on that. It was bad enough to write one letter, let alone two. But he drew another sheet of paper toward him and began again. After all, it wasn't too hard. He just copied the letter he had written home, leaving out, of course, the part about Annie. He was just signing his name when Denny came.

Denny leaned on the half door. " Come away," he said, " for a bit of a tramp."

" It's raining," said David.

" Och, never a bit of it," Denny assured him.

David looked doubtfully at the weather. It did seem to have let up, but everything was dripping wet. Still, Robert had bought him heavy boots like Denny's. There was no reason for him to be afraid of a little rain. " O.K.," he said. " But let's not go through the field where the bull is."

" Och, you're afraid of a bull," jeered Denny.

" But I'm not scared of fairies," said David.

" Whist now," said Denny. " You wouldn't want to be hurting their feelings, would you? " But he took the long way around, avoiding the bull's pasture. " And speaking of bewitchments and the like," said Denny, " I hear that Tidy John put a spell on your grandmother's Kerry cow."

" Who told you that? " asked David.

Denny shrugged. " I heard it around," he said.

" Well, it's not true," said David. " There's no such thing as spells, anyway. I don't believe in them, and my grandmother doesn't either."

"You're but a stranger in Ireland," said Denny, and didn't pursue the subject any farther.

Their steps turned naturally to the cairn. They climbed to the center of the mound and looked down into the place where the tree had stood. There was a fair-sized hole left, and David pushed in an exploring hand.

"I wonder what's down there," he said.

"Don't know," said Denny. "The Colonel said we weren't to touch anything."

"I bet you're scared," said David, who had not forgotten Denny's taunt about the bull.

Denny didn't answer. Instead, he put back his head and looked at the sky. "It's about to rain," he said suddenly.

"Don't change the subject," said David. "No one over here pays attention to a little rain." But the words were scarcely out of his mouth before a perfect torrent descended on their heads. "There's John Steenson's cottage," he gasped. "Maybe we'd better go there."

"The key is under the leek bush," said Denny.

Heads down, they raced across the field and crashed through the thicket. Then Denny stopped with a jerk. Music was coming from John Steenson's cottage. "The Little People," he whispered. "They've taken over the place."

"Let's look inside," said David and started on.

Denny caught his arm. "Wait now," he said. "They'll be angry if we burst in on them without warning." He lifted his voice in a quavering hail. "Hello, the house," he called and waited.

There was no answer. The music went on without a break. " I'm getting wet," said David, pulling away from Denny's grasp. He started to run again, and Denny followed reluctantly. The half door of the cottage was open, a peat fire burned on the hearth, and on the wooden bench in front of it sat Michael the Fiddler playing to himself. When he saw the boys, he lowered his bow. " The top of the morning," he greeted them calmly.

" And the rest of the day to yourself," said Denny a little grudgingly. He reached over the top of the half door and unfastened the latch. " And what might you be doing here at all? " he asked and stepped inside.

" And why wouldn't I be here," asked Michael, " when it was yourself that told me the key was under the leek bush? It was the day that you were so busy at the cairn, and I was in the thicket beyond."

" I wasn't talking to you," said Denny. "I was talking to the Little People."

" And sure I'm a good friend of the Little People," said Michael. " We are hand in glove, the lot of us. If you like, I'll tell you a story about the Little People that I had from one who was there himself."

It was raining. What could be better than to stay snug by the fire and hear a story? The boys settled themselves to listen.

" It was this way," Michael began. " There was once a poor fellow by the name of Rory O'Day that was coming home late one night after a hard day's work. He was that tired that he sat himself down beside the ditch for a bit of a rest, and all of a sudden he heard the sound of many voices singing together. Very sweet it sounded too. ' Sunday, Monday, Sunday, Monday,' they sang together, then rested before they sang it all over again. ' Sunday, Monday, Sunday, Monday.'

" Now mind you, it was grand music, and Rory was happy to hear it. But after a while it grew tiresome-like, hearing the same words over and over. ' Maybe they don't know any more,' said Rory to himself. ' Maybe they don't know the days of the week.' So when they stopped to rest the next time, he went on with it in his very best voice. ' Tuesday, Wednesday,' he sang. ' Tuesday, Wednesday.'

" Now it was the fairies that were singing, and mind you, it was the truth that they didn't know any more days of the week, and when they heard the new words they were as happy as Larry. They came over to Rory, and they picked him up as though he were a straw in the wind, and they carried him off to their palace. There they made as much of him as though he was the first man in the land. But after a while, what with the feasting and the singing and the dancing, he grew so tired that he fell asleep; and when he woke up he was beside the ditch again. But, would you believe it, he was dressed in a fine new suit of clothes, and in his pocket was a goldpiece that was more money than he had seen in his entire life before." Michael stopped to fill his pipe.

" That was a good story," said David. " Thank you very much."

" But that's not the end of it," said Denny.

" It is not," said Michael. " When Rory's story got about, there was a fellow named Jack Madden heard of it, and he decided to try his luck with the fairies. If

Rory can get a new suit of clothes and a piece of gold, he said to himself, sure I'm good for two suits at the least. So one fine moonlight night he sat himself down by the ditch and waited for the fairies. Pretty soon he heard them singing, 'Sunday, Monday, Tuesday, Wednesday.' Then they rested and started all over again. But Jack was a terrible rude fellow and without waiting for them to finish he bawled out, 'Thursday, Friday, Saturday.' The fairies were in a rage. 'Who spoiled our tune?' they shouted. They were on him in a minute and they pinched him and poked him and stepped on his toes until he cried out for mercy. And when morning came, there he was by the side of the ditch, his clothes all torn and not a sixpence in his pocket."

Michael took up his fiddle and began to play. "Sunday, Monday, Sunday, Monday," he crooned to himself.

It had stopped raining, and the boys stood up to go. "I liked your story very much," said David.

"Come again and I'll tell you another," said Michael. "But you wouldn't be telling the Colonel that I'm staying in the wee cottage, now would you?" When the boys shook their heads, he went on. "And I'll be giving you a bit of advice. 'Tis a dangerous thing to be digging in the cairn. The Colonel may be thinking he'll find a treasure there, but it's little good it will be doing him, for there's a spell on it. Leave it alone, my lads." He spoke so seriously, with such a gloomy face, that the boys felt a chill of apprehension.

"I knew it," said Denny. "I've felt it in my bones."

84

11

LYNN CAME BACK FROM DUBLIN BY HERSELF. HER
father's business had taken him to England, and he had
put her on the train for home before he left. The very
next day Denny came over with orders. The boys were
to come to Bride's Hill right away. Bossy as ever,
thought David, but he went all the same. He was
anxious to hear all about the Dublin trip.

" It's a grand place," Lynn told them. " But I did
want to go to England with Daddy," she sighed.

" I've never been to Dublin," said Denny.

" Nor I," said David.

" You should see the museum." Lynn's face brightened at the remembrance. " All the things they have
dug up and put there! We must get to work today on
the cairn. I'm sure there's treasure there as fine as anything in the museum."

" Your dad said you weren't to dig without him,"
Denny pointed out.

" Och, that," said Lynn. " It was only that the dear
man got a crick in his back and didn't like to admit he
couldn't keep up with us. He'll be glad to have us do
the work for him."

" He will not," said Denny. " And besides we've had a talk with Michael, and he says there's a spell on the place. No good will come of digging there, he says."

" Now, Denny," said Lynn, " how silly can you be? You know in your heart and soul that's all nonsense."

" I do not," said Denny stubbornly.

Lynn thought a minute. " Well," she said, "it will do no harm to have a look at the place. Come away now and we'll visit the cairn. But wait while I get my sweater."

No sooner was she out of the room than Denny spoke hurriedly. " I'm not going a step with her," he said. " She'll make us dig. You'll see."

" She's awful stubborn," said David. " But we might go to John Steenson's place and ask Michael to tell us a story."

" Michael said we weren't to tell that he's living in the cottage."

" That's right. Well, then, we'll just walk over to the cairn and back. She can't make us do anything we don't want to do."

" Can't she! " cried Denny. " She can indeed. I know her from ah to zed."

" Ah to zed," repeated David. " That's a new one."

" Don't you know your alphabet? " asked Denny.

" Oh," said David, " you mean *a* to *z*."

Denny was ready to put up an argument, but just then Lynn came in, struggling into her sweater, and they started off together. Denny had made up his mind. When they reached the crossroads, he turned the other way. " Mother will be looking for me," he mumbled.

Lynn opened her mouth to protest, but Denny's jaw

was set. She watched him hurry away. " Poor lad, he's the victim of superstition," she said with a shake of the head.

But Denny had known what he was talking about. As soon as they reached the cairn, Lynn went to the thorn-bush where they had left their tools. " Here," she said and handed David a spade. She picked up another and marched straight for the hole where the tree had been uprooted.

" But we weren't to dig without your dad," said David.

" We have to dig," said Lynn. " If we wait for Daddy, this place will never be cleared. We'll dig only in the hole anyway. We can't do any harm there." She shov-eled up a spadeful of dirt in a businesslike way as she spoke.

David had taken the shovel reluctantly, but he couldn't let a girl work while he stood around watch-ing. He began to dig too. It wasn't much fun digging, just the two of them. Even Lynn had to admit it. After a while she dropped her spade and sat down on one of the stone slabs. " There must be some way to get Denny over his foolishness," she said. " He was all right until that silly Michael set him off again. Were you there? What did he say? "

" He said there was a treasure buried there in the cairn, but that it wouldn't do us any good if we found it because there was a spell on it."

" A spell! " jeered Lynn. " What kind of spell? "

" I wouldn't know," said David. " But Michael be-lieved it, and so did Denny. Of course, I knew better," he added quickly.

" If Denny could just see the things in the museum, he'd change his mind," said Lynn. " They'd make your eyes stand out: amber beads and bronze swords and a stone ax like your grandmother's. No one had a spell cast on them for finding them. At least, I don't think so," she added a little uncertainly. " If we could find an ax now," she finished, " Daddy would be dazzled and entranced."

She jumped up at that and seized her spade again, and David, who had been happy to stop work, followed slowly. All this time he had been listening in hopes of hearing Michael's fiddle. Of course, he would never tell on Michael, but if Lynn found out by herself that he was in the cottage, she wouldn't mind, he was sure. How much nicer to listen to one of Michael's stories than to work all the time. He'd quit right now, he told himself, if he weren't ashamed to let a girl get ahead of him.

The earth, loosened by the tree roots, was not hard to dig. There were a good many large stones that they moved out of the way and so laid bare a fair-sized hole. " You get down in there," said Lynn, " and throw the dirt up to the top. I'll work over here at the side of the hole."

There was something about her that made her get her way every time, so David soon found himself in the hole, burrowing away at the bank and throwing out spadefuls of earth, just as she had directed. She worked as hard as he did, and the hole grew deeper and larger. After a while she came over to inspect.

" How are you — " she began, when suddenly the bank where she was kneeling gave way, and she slid

into the hole in a shower of dirt and stones. Her descent knocked David off his feet, and then they were both falling down, down. Half choked with dust, David was brought up with a jolt on what seemed to be solid rock. He scrambled to his feet and looked around. They were in a small underground room lined with stone slabs. Part of the roof had fallen in, dropping them to the floor. There was a queer dank smell in the place. It was dark and horrible.

"You would dig," said David bitterly.

Lynn didn't answer. She was lying down almost covered with stones and dirt. In the dimness her face looked pale and scared. She tried to get up, then sank back with a moan. "My foot's caught," she said in a small voice as she struggled to a sitting position.

"Hold everything," said David comfortingly. "I'll soon get you out." He began working with his hands to clear away the dirt, only to find that her foot was wedged between two stone slabs that had fallen from the roof. He caught his breath when he saw their size. If they had fallen on Lynn, she would have been crushed. "Maybe I can pry them apart," he said, half to himself. But they were too big. They refused to budge.

Lynn was not one to give up. "If I can get my shoe off, maybe I can wriggle my foot out," she said. She leaned forward and began to fumble with the shoelace, but dirt had worked into the knot. "I can't get it untied," she said. "You'll have to break it."

"Won't it hurt?" he asked anxiously.

"Never mind if it does," she said.

He gave a yank on the shoestring, then another. He could feel Lynn quiver, but she didn't make a sound. With the third try the shoelace broke. "Now," said Lynn, "take hold of me and pull." They heaved together, and Lynn's foot slid out of the shoe. She lay panting for a minute, then gave a breathless little laugh. "My shoe's gone. I like to go barefoot. This is my chance." She took off the other shoe. "How are we going to get out of here? " she asked, looking up at the opening which seemed very far above them.

David had been wondering about that too. The stones and dirt that had fallen in with them lay in a heap. " If we climb on top of this," he said, pointing, " maybe I could boost you the rest of the way."

" It's too far," said Lynn. " Your shovel is here. It fell in with you. Could you shovel the dirt into a higher pile? "

" I'll try," said David. Shovel in hand, he crawled to the top of the pile of dirt and looked around. It was lighter up here, but the opening was still far away. They'd never be able to build a pile high enough to reach the top. " Maybe I could jam the shovel into the dirt, and we could use it as a sort of ladder."

Lynn climbed onto the pile after him. " This isn't the place to go barefoot," she said and tried to laugh.

David looked at her. She had sunk to her knees and her head was bent. " I'm afraid I've hurt my foot," she said.

" Hurt your foot! " he repeated in dismay.

" It isn't because I'm a girl," she said defensively. " Boys get hurt sometimes too."

" Of course they do," said David. He drove the shovel into the dirt and packed more dirt around it. " Now, then," he directed, " put your foot in the hand-hole and lean on me. Up you go."

Lynn made a brave try, but her foot gave way beneath her weight and down she fell, the shovel toppling with her. " Ouch! " The cry was wrenched from her. For a minute David was afraid she was going to cry.

" Rest a little," he said, " and we'll try again. I didn't

91

ram the shovel in well enough, I guess."

" It's no use," said Lynn. " We're only wasting time. You'll have to climb out and get help."

" And leave you? " cried David. This was a horrible place. He couldn't desert her.

" It's the only way," said Lynn.

David thought for a minute. Now was no time to keep secrets. " Michael the Fiddler is living in John of the Rock's cottage," he said.

" Get him," said Lynn. " He won't want to come, of course, because he thinks the place has a spell on it. And maybe it has." Her voice broke on the words.

" Don't talk nonsense," said David gruffly, though the same thought had come to him.

" I won't," she promised. " Come on, get out of here as fast as you can."

David jammed the shovel in again, this time between two slabs of stone. " Give me a hand up, will you? " he said. He put a foot in the handhole of the shovel and carefully raised himself, Lynn supporting him as best she could. An upright of stone, forming part of the wall, was directly in front of him. He measured the distance with his eye, gave a strong push forward, and launched himself for the opening. His hands closed over the top of the stone, and he hung for a minute, all his weight on his arms. They were being wrenched from their sockets. He would have to let go. Then he felt Lynn boosting him. With a last wild effort he raised himself as Lynn pushed. He was over the top. His breath was coming in great gasps, and he was trembling. But he was in the open air again.

12

HE RAN CRASHING THROUGH THE THICKET. "MICHAEL! Michael!" he shouted. There was no answer. The cottage stood closed and empty. Michael was nowhere about. He turned and raced back to the cairn.

"Michael isn't there," he called down to Lynn. His voice trembled. For a minute there was no answer. "Lynn," he called again. "Do you hear me? I'll have to go and get Robert. Can you stand it that long?"

"I can." Lynn's voice was scarcely more than a whisper, but in a minute it grew stronger. "Go to Bride's Hill," she said. "It's nearer. Get Tom Toolin, the stable boy, and tell him to bring a ladder and the trap."

"A trap? What in the world for?"

"To ride home in, you goose," snapped Lynn. "I can't walk on this foot."

"Oh," said David. He remembered then that they called the two-wheeled carriage he had seen in the carriage house a trap. "I'll be back as soon as I can."

"Don't tell Mrs. Guilaland," called Lynn, "or anyone else but Tom Toolin. Cheerio," she ended bravely.

"Cheerio, yourself," said David.

He had never thought Bride's Hill was far away, but now as he ran he wondered if he would ever make it there. He seemed to be in a bad dream where his feet never got ahead. Once he had to stop to ease the pain in his side. Then he was running again. Tom Toolin was reading the paper, his chair tipped back against the side of the stable, but at the sight of David's face, he jumped to his feet.

"It's Lynn," gasped David. "She fell down a hole we dug and she can't get out. She's hurt her foot too. She said for you to come with the trap and a ladder."

He had scarcely got the words out of his mouth before Tom was backing Monaghan between the shafts of the trap. "Where is she?" he asked.

"In the cairn at John of the Rock's place," said David.

"In the cairn!" cried Tom. "She'll be fair perished and demented in that place." He brought the ladder and put it in the trap. "Up with you," he said to David.

Mrs. Guilaland came to the door. "What's going on here?" she wanted to know. "Where is Miss Lynn?"

"Lynn doesn't want her to know," said David in an undertone. He tumbled into the trap, and Tom picked up the reins. Monaghan took out of the stable yard at a gallop. They covered the distance to the cairn in no time.

"Is it yourself, Miss Lynn?" cried Tom, peering down into the dark hole in the cairn.

"Och, Tom Toolin, dear," came Lynn's voice in a wail, "please get me out of here."

"I will," promised Tom. In a minute he had set the ladder in place, and before David could believe it, he was climbing out again with Lynn over his shoulder. It had begun to rain. Lynn was crying softly, and David was very sober. They rode in silence, the rain sluicing down on them. Just as they turned into the stable yard, Tom Toolin spoke. " I'm thinking it would be better to leave the digging of the cairn to your dad," he said.

" It would, Tom Toolin," agreed Lynn in a subdued tone.

Mrs. Guilaland was waiting for them. " Whatever have you done to yourself? " she scolded. " Bring her in, Tom Toolin, and be quick about it." When Tom had carried Lynn to a chair in the house, Mrs. Guilaland knelt to look at the injured foot. It was swollen and already turning black and blue. " A fine sight it's going to be, and you soaked to the skin as well! Sit right there until I get hot water to soak your foot, and dry clothes to put on you."

She bustled away, and David, who had been standing hesitantly by the door, spoke quickly. " I'd better be going. I'm sure sorry you got hurt, Lynn."

" It was my own fault," said Lynn, " but please, please don't tell anyone."

Mrs. Guilaland came hurrying back. " 'Tis no place for us," said Tom Toolin.

" Thank you, Tom and David," called Lynn as they turned away. " Thank you with all my heart."

It was still raining, though not so hard. David didn't care. He was stiff and sore all over. He took his time going home and he was in no mood for talk when Denny rose from behind the fuchsia hedge. " Don't you know enough to come in out of the rain? " he asked Denny.

"It's only a few drops," said Denny. "I've been waiting here the entire day. We have to go to see Old McManus about this digging."

"What are you talking about?" asked David. "Old McManus can't dig. He can hardly walk."

"I don't want him to dig," said Denny. "I want him to stop the digging."

David thought about that. He didn't want to dig any more either, and maybe Lynn wouldn't after this, but there was her father. No one could stop him if he had made up his mind. And he certainly had. "Old McManus can't do a thing with Colonel McClintock," he said aloud.

"He'll have to stop the digging," said Denny, "or the entire county will be under the spell. The place is bewitched, I tell you."

"I wouldn't say that," said David. But his voice sounded unconvincing in his own ears. If Denny only knew about that horrid underground room and the time they had had getting out of it, he'd have some reason to think the place was bewitched! Lynn was right when she said not to tell anyone. This was worse than the cow. Secrets, secrets, thought David.

"Will you come with me to see Old McManus?" asked Denny. "I guess so," said David reluctantly.

"Tomorrow, then," said Denny and turned away.

Mrs. McManus was in the garden, picking peas. "And how are the warts?" she asked.

"Gone entirely, thanking you kindly," said Denny. "Is his honor inside?"

"He is," said Mrs. McManus, "and it's himself that will be glad to see ye. It'll take his mind off his troubles.

96

His rheumatism's that bad you'd hardly believe it."

They found the old man bowed over the fire. " And who is it that's come to see a poor old man with one foot in the grave? " he asked without turning his head.

" It's Denny Foley, your honor, and David Trent, come to thank you for curing the warts."

" Cured, are they? " said Old McManus, turning part way around, his voice sounding quite cheerful.

" Would you look at my two hands," said Denny proudly.

" Aye, clean as a baby's," said Old McManus, nodding his head. His eye fell on David. " And would ye look at the red cheeks of him," he said. " It's the fine Irish air has done it."

" We've come to you for a bit of help," said Denny.

" And to the right place," said the old man.

" It's this way. You know the cairn that's at John of the Rock's place." Old McManus nodded his head. " Colonel McClintock has bought it, and he's set on digging in it for treasure. Now Michael the Fiddler says — "

But he got no farther. Old McManus turned an angry face at them. " He can't do it! " he shouted. " What was John of the Rock thinking of to sell to the likes of him? That cairn has been untouched since the memory of man. Everyone knows there is treasure there, but there's a spell on it. If the treasure is dug up, there's three good men will die."

" Dear help us! " cried Mrs. McManus in alarm.

" What did I tell you? " said Denny, looking at David.

" Has the Colonel been tampering with that cairn? " demanded Old McManus.

When Denny didn't answer, the old man turned to David. " He's sort of cleaned it up some," David admitted.

" I might have known it," groaned the old man. " 'Tis the spell that's on me already. 'Tis what has been ailing me from the first. I'll be one of the three that are to go, and herself a poor widow woman."

At this Mrs. McManus set up a wail. " Dear help us all," she cried.

The boys were on their way home at last. They were both worn out, what with Old McManus' groans and his wife's tears. They had been able to leave only by promising to warn the Colonel not to dig.

" If he won't see reason," Old McManus had said, " send him to me, and I'll put the fear into him."

" They're crazy as a quilt," said David. " There's no spell on anything. They're making it all up."

" What do you know about it, you that have lived in America your entire life? " asked Denny. " When is the Colonel coming home? "

" Lynn said tomorrow," David told him.

" Let's go and see her now. No good will come of touching that cairn, and no knowing what she may be up to now."

David hesitated. " She hurt her foot and doesn't feel good. Maybe she wouldn't want to see us."

" There you are," said Denny in triumph. " The spell is working. That's what ails her."

Lynn was in her father's study, her bandaged foot propped up on a stool. Her cheeks were flushed and
98

her eyes were too bright.

" I have a cold," she croaked. " Mrs. Guilaland keeps taking my temperature. She won't let the puppies in here to keep me company because they're not trained yet. Everything is terrible." She caught David's eye. " Have you told Denny? " she whispered. David shook his head, and she drew a breath of relief.

" Old McManus sent word to your dad," said Denny. " He says you mustn't dig in the cairn any more, because there's a treasure there, and if you find it, it will be the death of three men in the parish."

" Och, Denny, how can you talk such foolishness? " said Lynn, but someway her words lacked the right ring to them. She's not so keen about digging either, David decided.

Denny went on without paying any attention to her interruption. " The spell has begun to work already. Old McManus, himself, has been took bad. He thinks he will be the first to go."

Mrs. Guilaland came into the room before Lynn could answer. She carried a thermometer, which she popped into Lynn's mouth. " You keep that in until I come back," she said and went away again.

" Maybe we'd better be going," said David.

" M-m-m," said Lynn, shaking her head violently. " Don't go," she mumbled out of the side of her mouth. So the boys stood around uncomfortably until the telephone rang. Lynn took the thermometer out of her mouth and answered. " Daddy," she cried, then listened a minute. Her face fell. " You can't come home? " she wailed. " You've got a cold? Och, dear help you, you're sick." Big tears began to splash down her

99

face. " I hear you. Yes, I promise. All right, Daddy. Good-by," she said and hung up. " He's sick," she told the boys. " It's the spell. That dreadful cairn. I wish we'd never seen it."

Denny gave a loud groan at this, but David spoke sharply. " Try to get some sense into your head. Your dad's got a cold," he told Lynn. " So what? You've got one too. A cold isn't anything."

" Do you really think he'll be all right? " asked Lynn, unexpectedly humble.

" Of course he'll be all right," said David. " Now, you'd better put that thermometer back in your mouth before Mrs. Guilaland comes back."

She obeyed meekly enough, but when Mrs. Guilaland came back she burst out with the news. " Daddy's sick," she wept.

Mrs. Guilaland took the information calmly. " You're feverish," she said after a look at the thermometer. " It makes you flighty. I'm going to put you straight to bed, my lass."

" We're just going," said David quickly, and the boys started for the door. Mrs. Guilaland went down the passage with them and saw them out. " I hope Lynn will be better soon," said David politely.

" She'll be all right," Mrs. Guilaland assured them. " Give her another day, and she'll be as right as rain."

They were by the study window when they heard a stage whisper. Lynn was leaning far out, beckoning. " David," she called, " come near and listen to me. Please," she whispered when David came close, " go fill in the hole we dug in the cairn. If there's a spell on the place, we've got to lay the spell. I'd go myself if I
100

could, but you know I can't."

" That hole is as big as a house," said David. " I couldn't fill it in. And besides, your dad will want to see that little room. He'll never give in to any old superstition, and you know he won't."

" I suppose you're right," said Lynn, " only I wish, how I wish, we'd never seen that place." She turned. " Yes, Mrs. Guilaland," she said over her shoulder, " I'm coming. I have to go," she told David.

" Don't worry," comforted David. " Your dad will know what to do. Everything's going to be fine. Cheerio."

13

" OLD MCMANUS HAS BEEN TOOK BAD," SAID OWNIE
Kern at breakfast. " They say he's not long for this
world."

Mrs. Hazlett shook her head. " Poor good old man,"
she said. " He and his wife have lived in that little
cottage as long as I can remember."

" Who will cure people's warts when he is gone? "
asked Robert.

" This is no time for jesting," said his mother re-
provingly.

" No jesting about it," said Robert. " Old McManus
is a great curer of warts. I remember the time that
James Carey, who has gone to New Zealand now, refused to sing in the choir because of his warts. Just to
hold up the hymnal in front of everyone at church was
more than he could bear. So off he went to Old Mc-
Manus and got a bit of folded paper and buried it
and — "

" That's enough," said his mother scandalized.

" And the warts disappeared," Robert went on,
" and James went back to the choir to sing like a bird."

Even Mrs. Hazlett had to smile at that.

" They say there's a spell on Old McManus," said Mary McInnelly.

" Mary, how can you be so silly? " Mrs. Hazlett began, then her eye fell on David, and she broke off in the middle of her sentence. " Davy, darling," she cried, " what ails you at all? "

" Nothing." David spoke quickly, but his voice was a mere croak. He was feeling awful. This talk of spells was bringing back the whole horrid experience in that dark underground room. Indeed, it had never really left him. He had dreamed all night about it and of Lynn crying because she thought Old McManus and her father were both bewitched. He knew the whole thing was nonsense, of course, but he couldn't seem to put it out of his mind.

His grandmother was still looking at him. " The lad's as white as paper," she said. " And I was priding myself on his rosy cheeks. What have you been doing to yourself over at Bride's Hill? That Lynn is always up to something. Is she too much for you? You'd better stop at home with me today."

The color rushed back into David's face. Any time I can't keep up with her! he thought indignantly. " I can do anything Lynn can," he said aloud. " Anyway, she's hurt her foot and has a cold. I'm not going over there today."

" Why not come and help us in the field," suggested Robert. " You've been neglecting us lately."

" Aye, we'll put you to work," said Ownie.

But his grandmother was not satisfied. After breakfast she took Robert aside. " The lad's got something on his mind," she said.

103

"You'd worry about the ducks going barefoot," said Robert, but he looked at David somewhat anxiously. "David is all right, but if there's anything troubling him, I'll find it out," he promised.

It was pleasant in the fields, with nothing to remind David of cairns and underground chambers and spells. The men made much of him, and his spirits soared. At noon Mary McInnelly brought the lunch and left them. Robert had not forgotten his promise to his mother. "Maybe you've been to see Old McManus," he ventured.

David nodded. "I went with Denny. He wanted to show Old McManus that his warts were cured. But I don't like this business of spells," he blurted out, looking at Robert.

"There's nothing to worry about," Robert said. "Remember the little Kerry cow," he added under his breath.

At the words a load rolled off David's shoulders. Of course, he knew there was nothing in this business of spells. The Kerry cow had proved it. Why had he forgotten? All at once he felt wise and grown up. He and Robert had a secret together.

"Maybe you have some knowledge about the spell on Old McManus," said Ownie.

It was all David needed, and the whole story came tumbling out. "And now Colonel McClintock is sick and couldn't come home yesterday, and Lynn has made up her mind that he'll be the second man to die because of the treasure." He looked at Robert for reassurance.

Robert smiled. "Did you find the treasure, then?" he asked.

104

" We didn't even look for it," said David. " The hole was awful dark and smelled funny, and Lynn hurt her foot, and we thought we'd never get out. I had to go to Bride's Hill and ask Tom Toolin to bring a ladder. I never thought of the treasure and I don't think Lynn did either."

Ownie had been looking sober, but now he heaved a sigh of relief. " It's the treasure that has a spell on it," he declared. " There's no curse for just digging a bit — provided you don't do any more of it," he finished warningly.

David was feeling better and better. " Lynn was plenty worried. Maybe I'd better go and tell her what you say, that is, if it's all right for me to quit work now," he said, looking at Robert.

" Go right ahead," said Robert gravely. " It's in a good cause."

Lynn was feeling very sorry for herself. " My foot's better and my cold is nearly gone," she said in answer to David's question. " I wanted to go for a ride on Mayo, but Mrs. Guilaland said no. She's silly, but I have to mind her when Daddy's away." Her face took on a worried look. " I haven't heard a word more from Daddy. He's sick among strangers, and it's all my fault." Her lip quivered. She was ready to cry again.

" Now look here," said David firmly, " Ownie Kern says that as long as we didn't find any treasure, we couldn't have stirred up any spell, and Ownie is awfully superstitious. If he's satisfied, you ought to be, especially since we don't believe in those old spells anyway."

"Only — " began Lynn, then thought for a minute. "That's right," she said at last, her face breaking into a smile. "We didn't find the treasure, did we? I never thought of that."

"You see, it's all right," said David. "What kind of treasure would it be," he wondered, " pieces of eight, do you suppose? "

"You're thinking of pirate's treasure," said Lynn. "That underground room was built long before there was any money in Ireland."

"No money? " asked David. "How did they buy things? "

"They traded things. Daddy says they would give bushels and bushels of stuff for any metal tool. You see they had only stone tools, most of them, and metal tools would be a real treasure to them."

"You mean the treasure could be only a little old ax or something? "

"It could be."

"But that's no treasure at all. It wouldn't be worth putting a spell on."

"Maybe it's all a mistake," said Lynn. " I mean spells and all. But I did hear that Tidy John put a spell on your grandmother's Kerry cow."

"He did not," said David.

"How do you know? "

"I know because I was there. That's how," said David.

"Tell me," demanded Lynn.

But David shook his head. " It's a secret, but I'll tell you this, the little Kerry cow wasn't bewitched at all."

Lynn was looking hard at him. He could tell she was

going to worm the story out of him if she possibly could. He steeled himself, but luckily the clatter of hoofs in the courtyard saved him from her questions.

" Where is her daddy's Irish rose? " called a cheerful voice.

" Daddy," shrieked Lynn and ran out to meet her father. The tears were running down her cheeks. " I thought you were going to die! I thought you were doomed," she wept.

" What ails the lass? " cried the Colonel in alarm.

" Old McManus said he'd be the first, and I thought you'd be the second," said Lynn.

" What kind of talk is this? " demanded the Colonel. He looked past Lynn to where Mrs. Guilaland stood in the doorway.

" She's had a bit of a cold and a fever," explained

Mrs. Guilaland calmly. " It always makes her flighty, you know."

The Colonel looked relieved, but Lynn was tugging at his hand. " Come away to the study," she said. " David and I have to talk to you." They started for the house. " Come, David," Lynn commanded, and he followed, very worried to be mixed up in the affair.

" Now," said the Colonel when the study door was shut, " what's all this about? "

" You tell him," said Lynn, looking at David. " You were the one who went to see Old McManus."

" Well," began David, trying to get his thoughts in order, " it was really Denny who wanted to go. He thought we oughtn't to work at the cairn, you know, and when Michael the Fiddler said it was bewitched, he got scared and said we had to go to see Old McManus about it. And Old McManus said if we dug up the treasure, three men would die. When he found out we'd been working there, he started to groan and said the spell was working already and he wasn't long for this world. And Mrs. McManus began to cry, and it was awful."

" Aye, it would be," said the Colonel. " Did you tell him we hadn't dug yet, and that he was getting ahead with his symptoms? "

Lynn and David looked at each other in silence and the Colonel's glance sharpened. " Have you been digging? " he asked.

" It was all my fault," said Lynn. " I made David dig, and we fell into a little underground room and I couldn't get out. David was very brave and went for help, or I'd surely be there still."

108

The Colonel's face underwent a good many changes while Lynn was talking. At first he was frowning, then at the mention of an underground room, his eyes began to sparkle, and by the time she had finished he was beaming. "An underground room," he repeated. "That's what I hoped for. Tell me about it."

So they began at the beginning while the Colonel listened, nodding his head from time to time. "Good, good," he kept saying. When they had finished, he asked all sorts of questions that neither of them could answer. "What kind of archaeologists are you?" he complained.

"All we wanted to do was to get out of there," explained Lynn. "After David left me, I kept my eye on the opening every minute in hopes of seeing him again."

"Well, it's good you didn't go messing about," said her father. "I can be sure that when we explore that chamber we are the first to do it in three thousand years. Think of it," he cried. "Think of it!"

"But what about Old McManus?" asked Lynn.

"I'll have to have a talk with the poor old chap," said her father. "I'll explain that the treasure isn't the kind he thinks it is, only some crude things buried with a chieftain. I'd better ask Dr. Steele to look in on him. He probably took a chill, and it's made his rheumatism worse. As to the cairn having anything to do with it, that's utter nonsense. I'm surprised that you could have been taken in by that," he said, looking over his glasses at Lynn.

Lynn appeared rather shamefaced. "Silly of me," she murmured. But she was soon herself again. "When are we going to the cairn? "

Her father looked at his watch. " I have an appointment right now. I must be off in a moment. We can't go to the cairn today, more's the pity. We'll make it tomorrow without fail. We'll see Old McManus first and pick David up on our way. How's that, my lad? "

" Be ready early," said Lynn.

" I'll be waiting," promised David. Now that the Colonel was back, he began to have an altogether different feeling about the whole adventure. He even looked forward with a kind of pride to seeing the underground room again.

Lynn evidently felt the same way. " It's a grand wee room," she was saying to her father.

14

How early is early? David was wondering impatiently when the Colonel and Lynn drove up in the trap. " Come away, David," shouted Lynn. " We're going to see Old McManus."

David bounded out the door, and his grandmother followed for a word with the Colonel. " I hear you've been under the weather," she said.

" Only a touch of the influenza," the Colonel told her. " Lynn was sick too."

Lynn shrugged cheerfully. " That was yesterday," she said. She turned to David. " Dr. Steele went to see Old McManus yesterday, and he's feeling better already. Daddy will set him right about the treasure, and then we'll be off to the cairn."

Monaghan was restive, tossing his head and stamping. " Up with you, lad," said the Colonel. David scrambled to his place, and the Colonel lifted his whip in salute as they drove from the yard.

" God bless all here," called the Colonel when they reached the McManus cottage. Unlatching the half door, he stepped inside.

" And ye too," answered the old couple.

"And how are you, man dear?" asked the Colonel.

"I can't complain," said Old McManus, a little grudgingly.

"It's a miracle," cried his wife. "Himself was so bad with the rheumatism ye'd scarcely believe it, but Dr. Steele has made a new man of him."

"It's these wonder drugs," said the Colonel. "If you have another siege, mind you call on the doctor for help. He'll fix you up. Now, I hear you laid it all on our digging in the cairn," he went on, going straight to the point.

"Aye," said Old McManus, "'tis well known that if the treasure is taken, it will be the death of three good men, and myself likely to be the first. I wonder ye would be after doing such a thing."

"Now, now," said the Colonel, "that's only idle talk. There's no treasure in that place, according to our idea of treasure. That cairn was built long before there was any money, when men used stone tools, and if a chieftain had the good luck to own a bronze ax or sword, they said it was treasure. Why, man, your poorest spade would be a jewel beside their best ax, and that buried these thousands of years."

"Then why should you be wanting to dig it up at all?" asked Old McManus suspiciously.

"Because I have a great longing to know what they had in those days. I want to be finding an ax like Mrs. Hazlett's or maybe an old sword."

Old McManus was still unconvinced. "Then why if there's no treasure, would they be putting a spell on the place?" he persisted.

"There's no spell at all," said the Colonel. "That

112

story was invented thousands of years ago to scare away any man who would want to steal what was buried there. A thousand years, mind you, is a long time."

" Aye, a long time," said the old man.

" Too long for a spell to last, though, mind you, I don't admit there ever was one. I'll show you all I find in that cairn. I give you my word. I wouldn't lie to you."

" I'm thinking ye'll dig there, anyway," grumbled Old McManus. " To find another ax like Mrs. Hazlett's wouldn't be such a bad thing at that." After a moment's thought, he added grudgingly, " Good luck to your work."

They drove away in high spirits. " I can't wait for you to see the wee room," Lynn told her father. " 'Tis a wonderful place."

David wanted to laugh. This wasn't the way she had talked before. But he didn't say anything. Since they had fallen in the hole, he had a different feeling about Lynn. She was a bossy character, but she was a good scout too and no mistake.

" Tom Toolin left the ladder, so we can get down into the room easily instead of falling in," Lynn was saying. " But it's dark down there; we'll need a torch. And a creel to carry off the dirt and stones, and a crowbar to pry up those big stone slabs. I want my shoe that's wedged between them. They're the best shoes I've owned in my entire life."

They left Monaghan and the trap in Tom Toolin's hands and set off on foot, laden down with all the things they might need on their " dig."

" How in the world did you manage to get out of

113

there, David?" asked the Colonel, peering into the hole in the cairn.

"If it hadn't been for David, I'd be there yet," said Lynn. "He just about saved my life."

"Lynn boosted me or I wouldn't have made it," said David.

"Well done, both of you," said the Colonel, "though, mind you, I won't say that you did right to disobey orders by working here while I was away." He didn't wait for an answer, but swung himself down the ladder. Lynn followed, and David, not too eagerly, came after. They were crowded close together, which seemed better somehow. Having the Colonel there made all the difference, and the ladder in the background was reassuring.

The Colonel was playing his torch about. "Och, it's better than I dared hope," he cried. The stone chamber had been hidden beneath the cairn. Its roof was made of overlapping slabs, some of which had caved in with Lynn and David. There was the big pile with the shovel still standing upright in it. But most of the stones were still in place in the roof. It was very neatly constructed. "Hello! Here's some pottery," said the Colonel, "food vessels, I think."

"But they're all broken to bits," said Lynn.

"They can be mended."

"But they aren't even pretty," said Lynn. They were only crumbled bits of brownish-gray stuff. "Not even as nice as an old flowerpot," she decided.

"Don't say that," said her father, examining a broken piece by the light of his torch. "See, there are spirals and zigzags like those on the stone outside. And look at this design in dots. Maybe thousands of years ago a woman pressed her fingers into the soft clay of a pot to make a decoration before she baked it. This is a splendid find."

" Look," said David suddenly, " there are pictures on these stones too."

The Colonel wheeled so quickly that he bumped into Lynn. " Hold it while I clear away some of this dirt," he said, and thrust the torch into her hand. " Spirals, triangles," he cried. " It's a human face, as I'm alive."

" How can you say that? " asked Lynn, staring unbelievingly at the queer markings. They certainly didn't look like a face to David either, though he didn't say so. Lynn held the torch for a while, but her father seemed to have forgotten everything in his enthusiasm. " My arm is breaking," she said at last. " I want to do something besides hold this old torch."

" Well," said her father reluctantly, " you can put the torch on the stone pile, and we'll pick up the broken pottery to take home with us. We can't do everything in a day. It will take a long time to examine this place thoroughly, and we need better light for it. Perhaps we might as well go now." He began collecting the broken pottery, and David helped him, but Lynn picked up the crowbar.

" I'm going to look for my shoe," she announced.

" Be careful now," warned her father. " Who can know what may be buried in that pile."

" I know my shoe is there," said Lynn. She pushed the crowbar under a stone slab and leaned on it. All at once it moved, then the whole pile collapsed, showering them with dirt, and the torch, dislodged from its place, rolled away. For a minute the air was full of choking dust. They could scarcely breathe, much less see.

" Where's the torch? " asked the Colonel, as the dust began to settle.

" Here," said David, picking the flashlight out of the dirt. Its light seemed to have grown very dim, but even so they could make out something new and strange that had been hidden by the pile of rubbish. It was a big oval stone, smoothed and hollowed out like a great dish.

" Is it a foot bath? " asked Lynn.

" It's a basin stone," said her father.

" What's it for? "

" No one knows. These basin stones are found in some of the underground chambers, but not all. Probably they had some special meaning, but we'll never know what. To think we've found one! " He was gloating over it, brushing away the dirt, studying it from every angle. " Cup marks," he cried as his fingers found two small round holes in the rim of the basin. " Some say they represent man — the two eyes, you know. But the mind of the man who made them is still a mystery to us."

He was still talking happily when the torch, which had been growing feebler by the minute, gave one last flicker and went out. The Colonel gave an exclamation of disgust, then sighed. " I suppose it's time to go," he said. " We've done all we can for one day anyway. Next time, with a proper light, we can settle down to serious work."

116

" Lynn, here's your shoe," said David, who had been grubbing about in the dirt.

" Good," said Lynn. " I'll be first up the ladder."

" David, you go next," said the Colonel, " and I'll pass the creel of pottery up to you. Careful, now. We don't want to smash any more of the pieces."

" I do wish Denny were here," said Lynn when they had gained the open air again. " It's too bad he is so superstitious."

" Ireland is a great place for superstition," the Colonel said kindly. " What with the rain and the fog and the mist taking queer shapes and the will-o'-the-wisp flitting over the bog, it's easy to believe strange tales. And these old cairns and cromlechs, with their stories of hidden treasure coming down from the beginnings of time, make fine talk for the country folk. David's grandmother would tell him the same."

" Och, David never believed a word of the spell," said Lynn. David opened his mouth to speak, but she didn't give him a chance. " I wish Denny would be as sensible," she sighed.

But when they reached Bride's Hill, Denny was there waiting for them. " Denny," shrieked Lynn, "you should have been with us! We found a little room inside the cairn, and no one knows what may be hidden there."

" But what about Old McManus? "

" We went to see him, and everything is all right with him. Old McManus is willing for us to dig, isn't he, Daddy? " she turned to her father.

" He is," said the Colonel. " You see, lad, the so-called treasure isn't exactly a treasure anyway, only

117

some old pieces of pottery and metal that have lain there for years and years. When I explained that to Old McManus and promised to show him what we found, he was satisfied."

"Dr. Steele has given him a wonder drug, so he feels fine," Lynn chimed in. "And now see what we found without even looking — a creel full of pottery that has to be mended. Daddy says it's maybe three thousand years old. And your eyes will stand out when you see our little underground room. You must come with us tomorrow. I give you my word there's no spell on it. Sure, I wouldn't lie to you. Och, Denny, come tomorrow, and you'll have the time of your entire life, I promise you."

15

"I DON'T SEE WHY WE CAN'T DIG BY OURSELVES," SAID Lynn, looking rebellious. " David and I found the little place without you."

"And a fine fix you got yourself into," said her father. " If it hadn't been for David here, where would you have been? No, you can't go digging in that cairn without me, and I can't work today. I have to catch up on the time that I've lost."

" Well, what can we do? " Lynn pouted.

" You can mend pottery."

" That old stuff," Lynn's tone was scornful.

" You won't be needed," said her father calmly. " David will work on it, and I see Denny coming around the corner of the house. He'll lend a hand."

" Denny," Lynn cried, jumping up, her ill temper forgotten. " Come in. We're going to mend pottery."

The Colonel gave them careful instructions. " I was sure we'd find pottery of some kind in the cairn," he said, " so when I was in Dublin, I brushed up on how to restore it. I found the best glue for putting the parts together and I laid in a good supply. Now you'll have to look carefully until you find two pieces that fit ex-

119

actly. Mind you don't make a mistake. They must fit perfectly. Glue them well, press them together, and set them in a box of sand to dry. The sand holds the pieces together until the glue hardens, but don't on any account get sand on the mended cracks or it will stick there and spoil the effect. Do you understand? "

" Of course," said Lynn. " It's easy. There's sand behind the stables. We'll get that first of all."

" Don't spill it about," warned her father. " Mrs. Guilaland will be cross if you do."

" She's cross already," said Lynn, lowering her voice. " She said she wanted to throw away the whole creelful of pottery. Imagine it! "

" We can't have that." The Colonel looked worried. " I tell you what, we'll keep everything in here in my study where it'll be safe from her. She knows she can't disturb this place. You can work on the table at the window if you promise to leave my things alone."

" We promise," they said together.

" Then I'll leave you," said the Colonel and set off for the stables.

Lynn and the boys found a shallow box, which they filled with sand and carried back to the study along with the creel full of dirty, broken pieces of pottery.

" Whatever are you doing with that rubbishy stuff? " demanded Mrs. Guilaland, who was waiting for them in the entry.

" Daddy wants us to restore the pottery for him," said Lynn. " We're going to work in the study so as not to disturb you."

" Och," groaned Mrs. Guilaland, " what's my housekeeping coming to with the likes of this going on under

my nose? " But she let them pass. The Colonel's study was forbidden ground, and it was seldom that she was allowed in there even to do the slight going over that he called cleaning. " The mess in there is past belief," she sighed.

Lynn didn't seem to mind her talk at all. She cleared the table at the window, dumping magazines, papers, books, pipes, and ash trays on the floor. Then she spread newspapers over the top, and the boys laid out the broken pieces of pottery.

" It will be like a jigsaw puzzle," said Lynn. " We just find the matching pieces and put them together."

But they soon found it wasn't as easy as that. The pieces were all very much alike and very dull and dirty-looking. It wasn't a bit like fitting together a bright picture puzzle. Denny was best at it. He seemed to

121

know by instinct just which pieces would fit.

" Look for the rows of little dents, and the zigzags," he told the others. " When they match, the pieces will go together."

" Daddy says those dents were made by the woman who made the pot," said Lynn. " She pushed her finger over and over into the soft clay before it was baked."

" Think of that, now," said Denny. " But you've got your pieces wrong," he pointed out, looking at Lynn's work. " The woman wouldn't put the dots hilter-skilter like that, would she, now? "

" I suppose not," said Lynn, beginning to hunt for another piece. " Denny," she said after a minute, " would you like to hear a true adventure story? "

" I would," said Denny.

" Well, then, I'll tell it to you — though David," she added kindly, " is the real hero."

" So that's how you hurt your foot and caught a cold," said Denny, when she had finished telling how they had fallen into the underground room. " Tell me now, didn't you think the spell had begun to work when you were down in that terrible dark place? "

" And why would I be thinking such nonsense? " asked Lynn with a great show of surprise. But after a minute she spoke again. " I won't lie to you," she said, " I thought of nothing else while I was alone down there waiting to be rescued. David was the only one who showed good sense."

" We-ll — " began David.

" Don't say it," interrupted Lynn. " You are the hero of the story."

By this time they had mended a few pieces, which

they set carefully in the box of sand to dry, Lynn giving a great deal of advice while they were doing it. " Put more sand under here," she said. " Mind you don't get any on the cracks."

" I know, I know," said David a little testily.

" They don't look like much," sighed Lynn, surveying their handiwork.

" Some of these pieces will fit together again," said Denny. " See, the fingerprints here look as though they'd match the ones on David's piece. Maybe they'll make one side of a pot."

Lynn stretched wearily. " Let's leave them to dry," she said, " and go out for a look at the pups."

" Hadn't we better pick up here a bit? " asked David, looking at the untidy room.

Lynn glanced around carelessly. " No," she decided, " we'll have to be working here a lot, and what Mrs. Guilaland can't see, her heart won't feel."

Mrs. Guilaland was scrubbing the kitchen floor. " Is that sand you have on your boots? " she asked Denny tartly.

He lifted his heel to look. " No, ma'am," he said politely, " it's just a bit of mud."

They hurried out of the house. " Don't mind her," said Lynn. " She is a great one to barge, but she has a good heart."

The puppies had grown. Farl of Bride's Hill and Sullivan Arms were tumbling over each other in a bid for attention, but the other puppy sat off by himself, a worried furrow over one eye. " Poor pet," said Lynn, " it's because he hasn't any name. No wonder he looks sad."

123

"How about calling him McManus," suggested David.

"And didn't Old McManus cure my warts?" said Denny. "It's a good Irish name."

"For a good Irish terrier," said Lynn. "McManus it is."

Colonel McClintock inspected the mended pieces of pottery. "You've done a good job," he told them. "We've got the makings here of at least two good-sized jars. We'll let them stand for a bit and go back to the cairn tomorrow. I'm going to spare a day to it again. Come over early, lads, and we can put in a good day's work. I'll speak to Mrs. Guilaland to give us an early breakfast so we can be off in good season."

"And you're not to be late, mind," Lynn called after the boys as they were leaving.

But as it happened both David and Denny were at Bride's Hill the next morning before the McClintocks were finished with breakfast. "It's not our fault," Lynn burst out. "Mrs. Guilaland wouldn't co-operate."

The Colonel came out chewing on a piece of toast. "She has no interest in archaeology, I'm afraid," he said with a shake of the head.

They had a good many things to carry with them: the lantern, two creels, a coil of rope, a piece of screening, and working gloves for everyone. On the way over, the Colonel told them the plan.

"First the dirt and stones that have fallen into the chamber must be cleared away. The place is too small for us all to work in. We'd only be in one another's way. I'll go down and fill the creels, and you lads can haul them up with the rope. Dump the dirt over the wire screening, and it can be Lynn's job to examine everything that won't go through the mesh. That means everything, lass, even the smallest bits of pottery."

" Axes and swords," said Lynn.

" And fairy gold," said Denny.

" Fairy gold would go right through the mesh and disappear," Lynn told him.

When they arrived at the cairn, the Colonel lighted the lantern and hung it from the top of the ladder. " Not too bad a light," he said, looking down into the hole.

" Denny hasn't been down there," said Lynn. " It's only fair that he should have a chance to look around."

But Denny backed away. " I can see fine from here," he said.

" We mustn't waste precious time," said the Colonel. " To your stations, men." He went down the ladder with the creel and rope, and very soon his voice, a little muffled, came to them from underground. " Haul away," he called.

" Be careful. Don't fall in," warned Lynn as the boys leaned over and began to pull on the rope. The creel came slowly, the Colonel pushing from below and all three pulling. " I won't fill it so full next time," promised the Colonel as it came bumping and thumping to the top. They had propped the screening over some stones, and the boys dumped the contents of the creel on the wire mesh and hurried back to the opening while Lynn settled down to inspect the load. At first it was great fun, but it was hard work, and no one was sorry when the Colonel's head appeared at the open-

125

ing. " Time for a break," he announced. " What have you found so far? " he asked Lynn.

" Nothing but some old broken bits. Quite nasty," she said.

" Don't say that," chided her father, who couldn't bear to hear a word against anything they found.

" Well they are," said Lynn. " I'm going down myself. I'm sure I can find something better than this stuff. Are you coming? " she asked the boys.

After a minute of hesitation, they followed her. By the light of the lantern they could see quite clearly the stone slabs that formed the walls of the chamber, etched deep with curves and spirals. The stones looked strange and uncanny. " I suppose they were some kind of magic," said David.

" Yes," said Lynn. " Daddy says it all had meaning. It was part of their religion, though nobody knows any more than that."

Denny, who had scarcely looked at the room, began shoveling dirt into the creel. It was almost as though he wanted to fill the creel as fast as he could so as to have an excuse to get out of there, thought David. And he didn't blame him, either. I wish the Colonel were down here instead of up there looking at what Lynn has sifted, he thought. Suddenly, there was a clinking sound as the shovel struck something hard, and Denny stooped to pick up a piece of blackened metal.

" It's a sword! " cried Lynn.

" It's broken. It's no good," said Denny.

" There must be more of it," said Lynn, seizing the shovel and beginning to dig. But Denny had already found another piece, widening into points on either

126

side, then tapering to a crude sort of handle. " Daddy," shouted Lynn, making a dive for the ladder, " see what Denny has found. It's simply glorious! "

" Too bad it's broken," said Denny.

The Colonel was looking at the pieces with a beaming face. " It was broken on purpose," he said. " When a great chieftain died, his sword was broken so that no lesser man could ever bear it. A sword," he cried, " a sword at last! " Brandishing the broken pieces over his head, he began to dance. The others stared at him in amazement, then Lynn's feet began to tap, and before they knew it, David and Denny too were capering madly about. Laughing, they threw themselves on the grass to catch their breath. " I think the spirit of that old chieftain must have got hold of me," said the Colonel ruefully. " I hope now I haven't done a mischief to my back," he added, feeling carefully of himself as he got to his feet. " I'm too old for such antics."

16

" NEXT WEEK IS THE FAIR AT BALLYNODE," said LYNN,
" and I'm going to ride Mayo in the junior race."

" Are you, now! " cried Denny.

" That I'd like to see," said David.

" You're going to," Lynn told them. " Daddy has
promised to take the Bride's Hill Antiquarian Society
to the fair. He says we've earned an outing. And I'm
sure we have. Would you look at the elegant pots we've
put together."

The boys' eyes followed hers to the shelf the Colonel
had put up especially for the things they had found in
the cairn. Two large misshapen pots stood side by side.
The cracks where they had been mended showed
plainly, and one had a large hole where the missing
piece had never been found. But that didn't take away
from the pride of the menders.

" They're a little on the plain side," admitted Lynn,
" but would you look at the fingerprint decoration. I'm
mad about those pots."

" I like them too," said David, " but I guess it's
mostly because we put them together."

" Restored them, you mean," Lynn corrected him.

David looked cross, but Lynn went on without giving him a chance to speak. " I wouldn't care for them myself," she said, " if I saw them anywhere else."

The bronze sword, still in two pieces, hung over the shelf. There had been a great discussion over it. " It ought to be mended," said Lynn. " It doesn't look right in two pieces like that."

But her father had stood firm. " That sword was broken for a reason," he said. " Who are we to go counter to a reason that is thousands of years old? "

" And the spell might work against us," said Denny, then blushed red with embarrassment.

" But it's no use at all in two pieces," cried Lynn, ignoring Denny's remark.

" I don't think it would be much use anyway," soothed David. " It's not as sharp as my mother's peeling knife."

So reluctantly Lynn had given in, and the sword, still in two pieces, now hung over the shelf, with the amber bead mounted on velvet below it.

" It's an elegant exhibit," said Lynn proudly. " Now let's talk about the fair at Ballynode. Daddy is going to see Mrs. Hazlett about David's going, and he'll have a word with your mother too, Denny."

" My mother will be willing," said Denny.

" My grandmother will let me go too, I'm sure," said David. " I'd like to see you ride."

" Is it a race then? " asked Denny.

" With jumping," said Lynn.

" Robert told me you were a fine horsewoman," said David.

Lynn looked gloomy. " There are those Costigans.

129

Five riders. And there's only one of me."

"Since when couldn't you stand up to any five of them!" cried Denny. "A March hare could never catch up with you on Mayo."

"I hope you're right," said Lynn. "Well then, let's go and have a look at the cairn. Daddy says it's safe now."

Their feet had worn a path along the familiar way past the cromlech and through the field. The place looked very different from the unkempt hillock that David had seen first. The grass was cut, the thistles pulled, and the fallen stones had been hoisted into place to make an enclosing circle. With the dirt and moss cleared away, many of them showed carvings of spirals and zigzags. Lynn led the way down the ladder into the chamber. The sun was so bright that they could see the carvings on the walls without lighting the lantern. The floor, cleared of dirt, was one great slab of stone, with the basin stone at one side.

"I wonder how they got it down here," said Lynn.

"The way we got the dirt out," said David, "just slogging away."

"My back aches just to remember it," said Denny. "It's a wonder the Colonel survived it."

A sudden cloud passed over the sun, and the little chamber grew dark. "It's a queer place," said Lynn with a shiver. "I don't like it much when Daddy isn't here."

"It's bewitched-like," said Denny.

For once Lynn didn't contradict him. "I'm glad there's a ladder," she said and started to climb, the boys close behind her. Rather out of breath, they came out into the open air, not quite looking at one another. Then Lynn drew a deep breath. " Of course we don't believe in bewitchment," she said.

" Let's go see Michael," suggested Denny. " He's back again."

" Does your dad know that Michael is living in John Steenson's cottage? " David asked Lynn.

" He wouldn't mind if he did," said Lynn with a shrug. " Come now, and we'll ask Michael to tell us a story."

Michael stood at the half door. " Come in, now," he welcomed them, " and I'll tell you how Paddy O'Brien brought a message to his cat from the king of the fairies."

Colonel McClintock drove them in the trap to Bally-node Fair; Tom Toolin had gone ahead with Mayo in the horse box. Monaghan was in fine spirits, passing everything on the road. Horse-drawn traps and brakes, here and there a small car, and more bicycles than they could count were all headed in the same direction.

" There's going to be a grand crowd," said the Colonel.

" I hope there won't be too many," said Lynn in a small voice.

Her father looked at her in surprise. " The lass is nervous," he cried.

" And who wouldn't be, thinking of those Costigans? " said Lynn.

The Colonel bridled. " The Costigans are a great riding family," he said, " but a McClintock is equal to the lot of them."

" And Mayo is a fine beast," put in Denny.

David wanted to add his word of encouragement, but he knew nothing of riding. He looked at Lynn in her breeches and tweed coat, her long braids topped by a stiff bowler hat. " We'll all be rooting for you," he said.

Lynn drew a deep breath when the fairgrounds came into view. Tents, looking white at least from a distance, had been set up where food was being sold, and crowds already milled about in noisy, good-natured confusion. The Colonel left the trap on the outskirts, and they made their way on foot past droves of sheep and cattle waiting to be judged. A prize bull stood in a flimsy stall, the rosette pinned on his head collar drooping over one eye.

Lynn stopped. " Och, the poor beast," she said, " his elegant appearance is destroyed entirely." Carefully she straightened the ribbon while David watched uneasily.

" That old bull could get right out and go after us," he warned. But the bull only turned his back in a bored sort of way as though ribbons were an ordinary occurrence in his life.

They found Mayo, looking sleek and beautiful, waiting at the paddock, Tom Toolin by his side.

" Where are the Costigans? " asked David.

" Yonder," said Denny, with a jerk of his head toward a group of girls chattering at the gate. They were fine red-cheeked youngsters, looking enough alike to be quints, but only three were in riding clothes. " They haven't riding pants enough to go around," said Denny. " They take turns wearing what they have."

" Miss Kate is to ride Gerteen Lass from Castle Cheyne in the ladies' race," Tom Toolin told them.

" Good luck, Miss Kate," he said and touched his cap as he caught her eye.

" We'd better be going," said the Colonel, " if we want to get a good spot to watch our lass! "

" Good luck," they cried, and David raised two fingers in the victory salute. Lynn managed to smile in return.

The Colonel chose a place near a hurdle banked at either side with greens. It looked terribly high to David. " Does she have to jump that? " he asked.

" It's not so bad from the other side," Denny assured him.

David couldn't see any difference, but there was no time to investigate, for the ladies' race was being called. Hunting ladies riding sidesaddle on beautiful mounts and a few girls, like Kate Costigan on Gerteen Lass, in breeches and tweed coats, were ready to compete.

" Gerteen Lass is a Galway horse," the Colonel explained. " She's used to stone walls. She can jump anything." And she could. Even David could see that. He found himself shouting at the top of his lungs.

But it was a different thing when the junior race was called. Later he wondered how he had lived through it. Two Costigans were entered against Lynn. Of course there were other riders, but to David no one else counted. From the beginning, one of the Costigans took the lead, with Lynn second, and the others strung out behind them. When they came to the first hurdle he had to shut his eyes. He heard the soft thuds as the horses landed, but he dared not look until Denny breathed, " They're over."

When he opened his eyes, a Costigan was still in the

133

lead, with Lynn close behind, and another Costigan on a gray, pressing them hard. One jump after another, and they still held their places. Then a groan went up from the crowd. The girl in front was down. It looked as though she would be trampled by the oncoming horses, but quick as a flash she rolled out of the way, and they swept past her. It was between Lynn and the other Costigan. David's heart was in his mouth. He could hear the Colonel breathing hard behind him. The last fence was right before them when the Costigan's horse swerved.

" Refused," sighed the Colonel. Like a bird, Mayo rose for the last jump. The race was won. Lynn, her cheeks flaming, the winning ribbon between her teeth, rode to the paddock.

" The luck was with me," said Lynn to the Costigans.

" Not a bit of it," they said. " You outrode us."

" A good race, well run," said the Colonel. " You've all earned your tea. Come along to the booth yonder."

" I'll not say no to that," said Kate Costigan.

" Have a care that you don't grow too heavy for your breeches," said a sister in sweater and skirt.

Kate shrugged good-naturedly. " That Joan only wants a chance to wear them herself," she laughed.

Lynn was walking with David and Denny. " Was I all right? " she asked.

" You were wonderful," was all that David could manage. He couldn't possibly have told her how he felt. But she seemed satisfied.

" And Mayo, the fine beast," said Denny.

The Colonel bought them sandwiches, the thickest David had ever seen, and hot tea in thick white mugs, and great slabs of ham. The girl who had taken the spill stood next to him. Her name was Meg. " So you come from America," she said. " I suppose you do nothing but ride around in huge motor cars over there."

" We can walk as far as anybody over here," said David a little huffily.

" Can you, now," said Meg. " No offense meant, I'm sure."

David felt apologetic. " I hope you didn't get hurt when you fell," he said.

" Why should I? " she asked. " It's only that Joan will have the next chance at my breeches."

" Hard luck," said David.

" No," she said. " Turn and turn about is fair play."

17

A LETTER CAME FROM ANNIE WHILE THEY WERE AT breakfast. Mrs. Hazlett read it and put it beside her plate without saying a word.

" What does Annie have to say for herself? " asked Robert when he saw his mother wasn't going to tell him.

" She says to expect her Saturday."

" Good," said Robert. " It will be grand to have her back."

" It won't be for long," said Mrs. Hazlett. " James is expecting her to sail in three weeks. It's all of a piece with his selfishness."

Robert gave a whistle. " Well! " was all he could say.

" It is not well," said Mrs. Hazlett. She stood up. " Come, Mary McInnelly," she said. " There is work to be done."

Robert and Ownie got up too and went silently off to do the chores while Mrs. Hazlett and Mary McInnelly started on a perfect fury of house cleaning.

Annie's name wasn't mentioned again, but on Friday, Mary McInnelly was sent up to clean her room, and David slipped up after Mary.

" What about this James Mackie? " he asked. " Do you like him? "

" He's a grand man, one of the best," Mary told him.

" Then why doesn't my grandmother like him? "

Mary gave the matter some thought. " She likes him and she doesn't," she said. " If he were to marry Miss Annie and settle down here, your grandmother would like him fine. It's the going away to Alaska that makes all the difference. Your grandmother is terrible set in her ways."

David went slowly down the stairs. He couldn't think of a thing that he could do to help matters. It looked as though the next three weeks were going to be very unpleasant.

" You'll have to drive to Killamena station to meet Annie," said Mrs. Hazlett to Robert at breakfast Saturday morning. " She can't walk all that way, carrying her bag."

" Ownie and I have a big day's work ahead," said Robert. " You'd better drive yourself and take the lad with you."

His mother pursed her lips. " I have work to do, myself."

" What is it that you can't set aside for a bit? " asked Robert.

" A woman's work can't be set aside any more than a man's."

" What is it that you have to do? " demanded Robert.

She hesitated, then her face set in stubborn lines. " It's my day to clean the silver."

Robert looked at her in astonishment. He even

137

smiled. " The silver can wait," he said. But his mother's face didn't change. Her mind was made up. There was no use in arguing. He pushed back his chair with an angry jerk. " Still holding a grudge against poor Annie," he said and flung out of the house.

Ownie hurried after him, and Mary McInnelly began nervously picking up the dishes. But Mrs. Hazlett sat on at the table. She poured herself another cup of tea with a hand that was not quite steady. Some spilled into the saucer, and she didn't seem to notice when a few drops fell into her lap as she raised the cup to her lips. Robert came back in a few minutes and stamped upstairs. David was waiting at the door when he came down again, in hopes of a ride to the station, but Robert passed him without a word.

" Come, David," his grandmother's voice sounded behind him, " you can help me with the silver."

She led the way to the parlor, and David followed. He hadn't been in the room since the night he got the fire tongs for Ownie, and he wasn't sure he wanted to go in again. But it was a nice room. The sun shone through the lace curtains, lighting up the fire irons and the tongs, now clean and shining. On the mantle over the fireplace were the two china dogs his mother had told him about. Their names were David and Jonathan, and when he was little he had someway thought that he was named for them, which was silly, of course, for he knew he was named David for his Grandfather Hazlett.

His grandmother went straight to the grandfather clock. " It's very old," she said. " It's been in the Hazlett family for generations. All the works are made of wood, and yet it still goes." She took a key from her pocket and unlocked a small door beneath the clock-

138

face. It swung open to show a tiny cupboard. " My safe," she explained. The silver, carefully wrapped in green felt, was stored inside. There were knives and forks and spoons and a silver teapot with sugar bowl and cream pitcher. " You can help me carry them to the kitchen," she told David.

They sat at the deal table, with the silver spread out in front of them, and Mrs. Hazlett began to polish the teapot. " My father, Thomas Cascaden, gave me this silver set when I was married," she said. " Not everyone has a set like this. I gave your mother the one that was in the Hazlett family. This was to be Annie's. But, no, she must go off to Alaska, and dear knows what use she'd have for it there."

" Is it just because she's going to Alaska that you're cross at her? " David blurted.

" Cross at her! " repeated his grandmother. " What nonsense is this? " She began to polish very fast, then her hand moved slower and slower until she sat quite still staring off into space. " Dear help me," she whispered, " maybe the lad is right." She began to polish again. " It's the last day of the week, and Robert has his hands full. I ought to have gone after Annie so that he could do his work. Och, it's my grandson that had to show me I was in the wrong." There were tears in her eyes as she looked at David. Then she smiled. " We must have a brilliament for Annie before she goes off to Alaska," she said.

David smiled back, though he had no idea what a brilliament might be.

A car was turning in at the gate, and Mrs. Hazlett ran to meet it. " Annie, my darling," she cried, and the two women fell into each other's arms.

If Mrs. Hazlett had shown no interest in the bridal plans before, she made up for it now, mapping out every detail from beginning to end. The time had come for David to be going home anyway, and he and Annie could travel together. It would be a wrench to part with them both, but they could take care of each other on the trip. A letter must be sent off to Miss Mooney about the change in plans. David's father and mother would meet them on the other side, and James Mackie would fly East for the wedding at their house. It was halfway between Alaska and Ireland. Annie, the dear child, would be married among her own people as was fitting and proper.

Nothing could be too good for Annie now. Mrs. Gillespie, the sewing woman, was sent for, and all day long the hum of the sewing machine filled the house. Mrs. Gillespie was a spry little woman, with gray hair drawn into a tight bun on the top of her head. She had never been away from the village where she was born, but she knew all about the kinds of clothes that should be worn in any part of the world.

" It's terrible cold in Alaska," she said. " It's wool you'll be needing, tweeds and the like of that. It was different, now, when Miss Irene O'Donnell went to marry her young man in Malaya. It was Irish linen for her and cottons and sheers. But woolens for you, Miss Annie." She looked at David over the top of her glasses. " So this is Miss Mary's lad. No great size to him, but strong built. Och, dearie me, many's the frock I made for your mother, and she the dear homely thing too."

Homely! David felt a rush of anger. " I'll have you know that my mother isn't homely. She's very pretty," he cried.

140

The women looked their surprise at this outbreak, but it was Annie who set him right. " Mrs. Gillespie didn't mean homely the way you thought," she explained. " She meant home-loving. Your mother is home-loving and pretty too."

" Oh," said David, embarrassed. " I'm sorry."

They all laughed then, though David was hot with embarrassment.

" 'Tis a good lad that speaks up for his mother," said Mrs. Gillespie. Then she went back to woman's talk. " You'll be getting married at Miss Mary's house in the States, I hear. You'll want a good silk for that, and it'll do fine for the brilliament here too. Tell me now, what will you be serving for the collation? And is it to be a knife-and-fork tea? "

David was glad to hear Denny's hail from the yard. " Let's go over to Bride's Hill," he said. " All they can talk about here is clothes and brilliaments."

" Is it true that your grandmother is serving a knife-and-fork tea? "

" How do you know so much? I just heard of it this minute."

" 'Tis the talk of the entire world," Denny told him. " But I wonder that you'd be asking Archie McDermott to play the flute for you. He can't compare with Michael the Fiddler, and Michael your true friend too! "

" It's the first I've heard of it," said David.

" Archie McDermott is a skellum," said Denny. " He'd be no addition to a party. But Michael the Fiddler is a terrible nice fellow and twice as good when it comes to a dance tune."

When they reached Bride's Hill, Lynn agreed with Denny. " It would be a sin and shame to have that Ar-

141

chie McDermott play for the brilliament. You must see to it, David, that Michael the Fiddler is the one who is chosen."

" But I haven't anything to say about it," protested David. " I didn't even know there was going to be any music until Denny said so."

" You know now — " said Lynn.

" Sure," David admitted, " but — " Lynn was looking at him. " I suppose I could ask Robert," he finished weakly.

" You must," said Lynn.

There she goes, thought David, bossy as ever. And there was no use arguing with Lynn. " I'll see," he said.

" That's taken care of," said Lynn, getting to her feet. " Now Daddy is waiting to see David."

" To see me? " asked David. " What for? "

" You'll find out," Lynn told him. She led the way to the study, where the Colonel was working at his desk. He stood up and looked at them over the top of his glasses.

" Ah, David, lad," he said, " there you are." He stopped and cleared his throat. There was a moment of silence. David looked from one to the other. They were all very serious. What could it be about? The Colonel was speaking again. " In behalf of the Bride's Hill Antiquarian Society," he said, " I take pleasure in presenting this token of our friendship and regard," and taking a long roll of paper from the desk, he handed it to David.

" Open it, open it! " cried Lynn excitedly. " It's a rubbing of the stone in the cairn. We plastered wet paper over it, and Denny and I rubbed it all over with

142

India ink. Then Daddy went over it again to be sure every bit was covered. It's really elegant. Open it."

But David was too overcome to do anything, so Lynn took the scroll from him, slipped off the green ribbon that bound it, unrolled the paper, and held it out for him to see. There were the spirals and triangles they had learned to know so well, copied perfectly in every detail.

" It's a man's face," said Lynn. David looked again, and sure enough, two dark spots in the middle of the spirals might really be eyes. Lynn was still talking. " Now read what it says," she said.

David made a real effort and began to read:

143

" The Bride's Hill Antiquarian Society
presents to our friend and fellow worker,
DAVID HAZLETT TRENT
this rubbing in memory of a happy summer.
Lynette McClintock
Dennis Foley
W. St. George McClintock "

They were looking at him with eager faces.
" Thanks, thanks an awful lot," said David soberly.
" It's — it's just about the nicest thing that ever hap-
pened to me."

18

THE GREAT BRILLIAMENT WAS SET FOR THE NIGHT BE-
fore Annie's and David's leaving. " We'll make a night
of it," said Robert, " and take the early train in the
morning." For it was decided that he would go with
them across the Irish Sea to Liverpool to put them on
the ocean liner for America. No one could talk of anything but the brilliament in the meantime.

Ownie Kern pretended to grumble. " It's a pity," he
said, " that James Mackie should have planned Annie's
flitting with the summer's work not done. It's no time
for Robert to be going off to Liverpool."

But even the thought of being shorthanded could
not put Mrs. Hazlett out of humor. " Mary McInnelly
can help in the field, and perhaps Tidy John will give
us a lift."

" Not Tidy John," said Ownie quickly. " He's no
good except with the slane," he explained when he saw
Mrs. Hazlett's look of surprise.

But for all of Ownie's grumbling, he was looking forward to the brilliament along with everyone else. The
whole countryside was invited. Annie had grown up
among them, and everyone wished her well. The sew-

ing finished and the trunks packed, even to the silver service, it was time to think of refreshments, and the good smell of baking ham and currant cakes filled the air. David hung about, his nose twitching, and he sampled everything that came his way.

" What have you done about the music? " Mrs. Hazlett asked Robert.

" I thought we'd get Jimmy Tiffin with his accordion," said Robert.

" Can he be trusted? " asked his mother. " With Jimmy, it's always ' Come day, go day, I wish it was Sunday.' We don't want to be left in the lurch."

" It's not often Jimmy gets the chance to play for an all-night affair," said Robert. " He said he'd be glad to come."

" There's no one else," said Annie, " unless we get Archie McDermott, and he would ask the world and all for his playing."

" There's Michael the Fiddler," David spoke up, remembering his promise to Lynn and Denny.

But his grandmother shook her head. " Och, that Michael," she said. " He's no better than a tinker."

David said no more. Even Lynn, he thought, couldn't have given an answer to that one. Robert went off to clinch the bargain with Jimmy, and things were left that way until the very day before the brilliament. " Have you seen Jimmy Tiffin lately? " Annie asked Robert.

" Jimmy promised," said Robert, but as he looked at Annie's anxious face he gave in. " I'll just step around and see him if you like. David, do you want to come too? "

" Don't be long now," said Mrs. Hazlett. " There are

a thousand and one things to be done, and we need your help to set up the trestle tables in the parlor for the tea."

" We'll be back in a moment of time," Robert promised cheerfully.

Jimmy Tiffin lived in a run-down cottage on the edge of town. In the garden patch a few turnips and potato vines struggled in a wilderness of weeds. The half door swung by one hinge, and David could look into the kitchen where a hen was picking up crumbs from the floor. An untidy woman, with a baby in her arms and an older child clinging to her skirt, answered Robert's call.

" Good morrow, is Jimmy at home? " he asked.

" He is not. "

" Where is he, then? "

" He's gone on holiday."

" And when will he be back? " asked Robert in alarm.

The woman shrugged. " The dear knows," she said. " A week or so, I expect. He was going to the west a-playing his accord-een."

" But he promised to play for Annie's brilliament to-morrow," cried Robert.

" Did he indeed," said Mrs. Tiffin. " Now that's too bad, and Miss Annie, the fine lass too, and going off to Alaska, poor soul — "

But Robert wasn't listening. He had turned and was striding down the path before she was half through, walking so fast that David had to run to keep up. " What are you going to do now? " David asked.

" I'll have to go to Archie McDermott's," said Robert with a scowl, and not another word was spoken until they reached Archie's place. It was as neat as Jimmy's had been untidy. His spotted horse was tied to the fence, and Archie himself was hoeing in the potato patch. Robert went straight to the point. " I've come to ask you, Archie McDermott, to play your flute at the brilliament tomorrow."

Archie took off his cap and scratched his head. " I might be saying yes to that, and again I might be saying no."

" And why would you be saying no? "

" 'Tis late in the day to be asking me. I might have other plans."

" Have you, then? " asked Robert.

" I wouldn't say I had," said Archie, " but I'm not so young as I once was, and my wind gives out once and again." He gave Robert a crafty look. " I might be having to ask a bit extra for my services."

" How much? " asked Robert. He was prepared to pay well, but the price that Archie named brought an angry snort. " It's highway robbery," he cried.

Archie's jaw was set. " Nary a whiff will I blow for less," he said.

" You'll not be getting it from me," said Robert, and forgetting everything that was at stake, he stamped away. But he hadn't gone far before he stopped in dismay. " Dear help me! " he cried. " I must have been demented. I'll have to go back and eat humble pie, though I'm heartsore to do it." He stood wavering in the middle of the road, the picture of distress.

" You could ask Michael, couldn't you? " David spoke diffidently.

" Michael," Robert said softly. " Michael," he re-

148

peated and started walking again. " The womenfolk
would never hear to it, but wait now. What if we didn't
tell them? It would be time enough for them to know
when the party was in full swing. Can you keep it to
yourself? " He looked at David.

" I never told about the Kerry cow," said David.

" You did not," Robert agreed. " Shake on it." Standing in the middle of the road, they shook hands
solemnly. " Now where, I wonder, would I be finding
Michael? It would be a fine kettle of fish if he has gone
on holiday too."

" He hasn't," said David. " He's living in the house
that used to be John Steenson's, John of the Rock, you
know."

Robert laughed. " For a lad that's from the States,
you seem to know what goes on here."

Michael was at home. " The kettle is on the boil.
Will you have a dish of tea? " he invited hospitably.

" Thank you kindly," said Robert. " We can't stop.
I've come to ask a favor. Will you play your fiddle for
the brilliament tomorrow? As to price, I'll make it
worth your while."

Michael didn't hesitate. " Och, I'll be only too proud
to," he said.

David was beaming. Lynn would have to admit that
he had done a good job, though really it had been just
good luck. But looking at his friend, he began to have
misgivings. There was a jagged hole in Michael's pants,
and his sweater was out at the elbows. His clothes
looked as though he had slept in them, which he probably had. " No better than a tinker," David's grandmother had said, and though David had never seen a

149

tinker, he was afraid it might be true.

"We want this to be the finest party in the world for our Annie," said Robert. "Everyone will be dressed in his best." He hesitated. "I could give you a pair of pants and a shirt." He broke off, embarrassed.

"Now, what could be fairer than that?" said Michael. "And maybe a necktie to wear at the start, before things begin to warm up. Shall I be walking along with you to get them?"

"No, no," said Robert hastily. "I'll get them to you." They left Michael then, but they were well away from the house before he spoke again. "Saved by a hair," he sighed. Then he broke off. "If it isn't that skellum, Archie McDermott, coming to meet us."

"Och, there you are," Archie greeted them. "I was just after looking for you." He lowered his voice confidentially. "I've been thinking that seeing your mother is such a fine lady, and Miss Annie that popular, and yourself my good friend, I could come down a wee bit on my price."

"I wouldn't be asking you to do that," said Robert, "and besides I've made other arrangements." He gave a stiff nod and started on.

But Archie was not to be put off so easily. "And what will you be doing then with Jimmy Tiffin gone off to the west?" he demanded.

"We'll be doing fine," said Robert, and left Archie staring after him in surprise.

"How are you going to get the clothes to Michael?" asked David.

"That I don't know," said Robert, "what with the women all over the place and myself at their beck and call. But we couldn't be letting Michael come to get them. It would never do."

" I could take them," offered David. " I could say I was going over to Bride's Hill, or something."

But Robert shook his head. " It's yours and Annie's last day with the family. They'll be expecting us to go nowhere at all. We've stayed away too long as it is."

They were still thinking of ways and means when they reached Slieverow House, and Denny rose up from the stone behind the fuchsia hedge. " Denny will do it for us, won't you, Denny? " said David.

" Anything at all," said Denny.

" Michael's going to play," said David proudly, " but we have to get some clothes for him to wear. Will you take them to him? "

" Sure I will," said Denny.

" Wait here, then," said Robert, " while I hunt them out. We don't want the womenfolk to know. I'll go up and put some clothes out on the bed and come downstairs. David, you are to get them as soon as you see me engaging my mother and Annie in the parlor. Sneak them out to Denny, and mind you don't let anyone see you. If it's found out about Michael beforehand, there would be an end to all peace and quiet."

Annie was watching for them. " Did you see Jimmy? " she called from the doorway.

" Everything is all right," Robert assured her.

" You were gone so long that my heart misgave me," said his mother, " and we waiting to set up the tables in the parlor."

" First, I have to take off this shirt," said Robert. " I'm perishing with the heat! " He made for the stairs,

151

and David, listening, could hear him moving about up in his room.

" Now what is he up to? " groaned Mrs. Hazlett. " Mary McInnelly, you go in and start moving the furniture back against the wall, and, Annie, you can help her."

Robert came whistling down the stairs. " At your service," he said, and taking his mother by the arm, he whisked her away to the parlor after the two girls. At the doorway he turned to give David a wink, and David ran for the stairs. A roll of clothes and a pair of shoes were laid out on Robert's bed. He caught them up and started down again, but his heart jumped into his mouth when he heard Annie's voice.

" I'll just go to the scullery and fetch them myself," she said and started down the hall.

" No, no," called Robert, " come back here now and give me a hand with this trestle. Everything else can wait on this."

" A man must always have his own way," said Annie. But she went back into the parlor, and after a moment's delay, David stole softly down the stairs. He looked uneasily toward the parlor, but Robert was making a great to-do, shoving furniture about and giving so much advice that the women had no time for anything else.

Once out in the yard, it was plain sailing. He thrust the bundle into Denny's arms. " Here," he said breathlessly, " please take it to Michael, then be sure to tell Lynn that everything's all right."

19

" Now, DAVID, LAD," SAID HIS GRANDMOTHER, " WHEN it's your bedtime, you must go upstairs and lie down on my bed."

" But I want to stay up like everybody else," David objected.

" Your mother wouldn't thank me for letting you do that," said his grandmother, " when you're starting on a journey the next day."

" But how can I sleep with all the noise down here? " asked David.

" You can rest," his grandmother told him. David said no more, but his mind was made up. Someway or other he was going to stay up all night along with the rest of them at the brilliament.

They were at the table, having a hasty bite of supper on the afternoon of the great day. " Don't dawdle with your food," said Mrs. Hazlett. " No knowing when the guests will begin to arrive."

" They won't be early when it's an all-night affair," said Robert, helping himself to another soda farl.

"If that isn't just like a man," said Annie, starting to clear the table.

" Have it your own way," laughed Robert and stood up, munching. But Robert was right. There was no need to hurry. Everything was in spick-and-span order long before the first guests arrived. They came in twos and threes, and then whole families, until the house was full and people spilled out into the yard.

" Where is Jimmy Tiffin? " Mrs. Hazlett asked in an anxious undertone.

" It's early yet," said Robert.

" It would be a fine how-de-do if he didn't come," worried his mother. " I told you he couldn't be trusted."

" Now don't worry," said Robert.

" You're sure Jimmy is coming? " whispered Annie a little later.

" You'll have your music, never fear," said Robert. But he was glad when Colonel McClintock came with Lynn and Denny and he could turn from his sister to greet them. The Colonel had been a great traveler in his day, and he began to tell the company stories of what Annie and David could expect on an ocean voyage.

" Where's Michael? " Lynn asked David in a whisper.

" I wish I knew," said David. " If he doesn't come soon, we're sunk."

" He's coming," said Denny. " He was at the barbershop for a haircut. He'd never miss the fun."

But after a while even Denny began to look worried, and Robert could no longer meet his mother's eye. Annie kept casting accusing glances his way. Soon the guests would be wondering too. " Could you go and

154

find him, Denny? " asked David. Then there was a stir at the door, and Michael himself stood there. His black hair was smooth, his beard trimmed. His shirt gleamed white against his bright tie, and under his arm he carried his fiddle.

" God save all here," he said in a deep voice.

" And you too," said Mrs. Hazlett as graciously as though she had been expecting him. The guests joined in a polite murmur.

" Och," cried Robert. " I'm that glad you've come. Tune up, man. Give us a waltz to start with."

Mrs. Hazlett led off the first dance with Ownie Kern; Colonel McClintock chose Annie as his partner, and Robert took Mary McInnelly, who was so overcome by the honor that she went off into one fit of the giggles after another. One dance was all that Mrs. Hazlett, Annie, and Mary had time for. After that their hands were full with the knife-and-fork tea. The guests came and went to the parlor in relays, and as soon as one tableful finished, others took their places.

Lynn, David, and Denny, their feet tucked under them, watched the dancers. Sweat was pouring down Michael's face, and he stopped to take off his tie and open his shirt collar, then fell to playing again. A square dance was in progress, the dancers giving way to shouts and squeals, stamping feet and swirling skirts. A double hornpipe followed, and then a girl did a solo jig.

" It's Meg Costigan," said Lynn. " Isn't she the elegant dancer! "

Annie was making her way toward them along the side of the room. She took Lynn by the hand. " You too, lads," she said to the boys, and led them to the supper table. The Colonel had already eaten and was engaged in lively conversation, but when the children had eaten he stood up.

" Come, lass," he said. " It's high time we were going. We'll drop Denny off at his house."

" Not yet," begged Lynn.

" I've promised Annie and David we'll be at the station to see them off," said her father. " You'll have to get some sleep first."

When Lynn and her father and Denny had gone, David was on his own. Feeling a little guilty at disobeying his grandmother's plan for him to lie down on her bed, he slipped back to find the company was singing to Michael's accompaniment. " Now then," someone shouted when the song was done, " give us a story, man dear."

David leaned his head against the wall to listen. " Sunday, Monday, Sunday, Monday," Michael's voice droned on. " Tuesday, Wednesday — "

Mary McInnelly was shaking him. " Wake up, Davy," she cried, " it's time to leave."

David sat up with a start. It was morning. The guests stood quiet as Annie in her new blue going-away suit came down the stairs with her mother. Robert was behind them carrying the suitcases.

" Here, give us the bags." Eager hands reached for them. Robert gave them up and turned to his sister. Hand in hand, Robert, Annie, David, and his grandmother set out to walk across the fields to the station, all the guests following them. They walked in a shining world where every leaf and blade of grass glittered in

156

the morning dew. The bright-blue smoke of peat fires rose straight up from cottage chimneys.

" It's a good sign," said Mrs. Hazlett. " When the smoke goes straight up, it means fair weather. You'll have a good crossing of the Irish Sea."

Annie looked about her with a sigh. " I will remember this morning to my dying day," she said.

At the station Michael struck up a tune. There was to be no sad leave-taking. They were all singing when the train came in. There was a minute for Annie to kiss her mother. Then Colonel McClintock spoke for them all.

" 'May the road always rise with you, may the wind always be at your back. And may God always hold you in the hollow of his hand.' "

" Amen to that," chorused many voices.

Annie stepped aboard the train, and David and Robert followed her. Amidst shouted good wishes the train pulled out of the station. Annie was on her way to Alaska, and David was going home.

Biography of Elizabeth P. Fleming

ELIZABETH P. FLEMING was born in Morioka, Japan, of missionary parents, the first foreign baby in that region. She came to this country while still young and received her education in the United States.

Mrs. Fleming was graduated from Teachers College, Fredonia, New York, and taught school until her marriage, when she moved to Chicago. She now lives in Oak Park, Illinois. She is a ceramic artist, with a kiln in which she fires her own pieces. She likes to garden, to play the piano, and to sew. Her favorite hobby is designing and embroidering gay animals on squares that she pieces together into picture-book quilts for children in the hospital.

The land of her birth has always held a peculiar charm for her. Her first book, *Gift from the Mikado,* is a true story of her family's life in Japan. It was chosen as a selection of the Weekly Readers' Children's Book Club. Her second story, *Redcloud & Co.*, was set in the state of Wisconsin, where Mrs. Fleming and her family have spent many happy vacations.

Mrs. Fleming is also familiar with the Irish scene. Her husband was born in Ireland and, as a little boy, spent his summers on his grandmother's farm in southern Ireland. Here he heard many stories from the country people about the great stones set up by prehistoric men. Mrs. Fleming has spent some time in Ireland and has made a study of the history of the stones and of the stories about them that she gives in this book about Ireland.

4708